"I'm...   want a big family."

"Yes, I want a big family," Hank replied. "Kin—blood ties—have always meant everything to me."

"Blood ties," she repeated softly. "You must wonder at me spending so much time and energy on other people's children."

"I admire you for it. It's not easy for many folk to step outside the pull of biological ties." He shook his head. "Especially hard for men somehow."

"I think it's an ego thing. Heirs. Dynasty. Immortality." She'd developed an edge to her words.

Hank puzzled over the new underlying anger in her tone of voice. Up until now, anger wasn't an emotion he would have associated with the indefatigable Miss Little. He wondered what experience had pushed her to it.

And what else could get her blood heated…?

Dear Reader,

Silhouette Romance is proud to usher in the year with *two* exciting new promotions! LOVING THE BOSS is a six-book series, launching this month and ending in June, about office romances leading to happily-ever-afters. In the premiere title, *The Boss and the Beauty,* by award-winning author Donna Clayton, a prim personal assistant wows her jaded, workaholic boss when she has a Cinderella makeover....

You've asked for more family-centered stories, so we created FAMILY MATTERS, an ongoing promotion with a special flash. The launch title, *Family by the Bunch* from popular Special Edition author Amy Frazier, pairs a rancher in want of a family with a spirited social worker...and *five* adorable orphans.

Also available are more of the authors you love, and the miniseries you've come to cherish. Kia Cochrane's emotional Romance debut, *A Rugged Ranchin' Dad,* beautifully captures the essence of FABULOUS FATHERS. Star author Judy Christenberry unveils her sibling-connected miniseries LUCKY CHARM SISTERS with *Marry Me, Kate,* an unforgettable marriage-of-convenience tale. *Granted: A Family for Baby* is the latest of Carol Grace's BEST-KEPT WISHES miniseries. And COWBOYS TO THE RESCUE, the heartwarming Western saga by rising star Martha Shields, continues with *The Million-Dollar Cowboy.*

Enjoy this month's offerings, and look forward to more spectacular stories coming each month from Silhouette Romance!

Happy New Year!

Mary-Theresa Hussey

Mary-Theresa Hussey
Senior Editor, Silhouette Romance

Please address questions and book requests to:
Silhouette Reader Service
U.S.: 3010 Walden Ave., P.O. Box 1325, Buffalo, NY 14269
Canadian: P.O. Box 609, Fort Erie, Ont. L2A 5X3

FAMILY
BY THE BUNCH

Amy Frazier

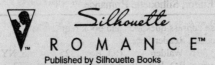

Silhouette

R O M A N C E™

Published by Silhouette Books

America's Publisher of Contemporary Romance

To my daughter, Sarah,
whose generosity of spirit
belies her age.

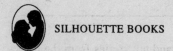 SILHOUETTE BOOKS

ISBN 0-373-19347-5

FAMILY BY THE BUNCH

This edition published by arrangement with Harlequin Books S.A.

® and TM are trademarks of Harlequin Books S.A., used under license.
Trademarks indicated with ® are registered in the United States Patent
and Trademark Office, the Canadian Trade Marks Office and in other
countries.

Printed in U.S.A.

Books by Amy Frazier

Silhouette Romance

Family by the Bunch #1347

Silhouette Special Edition

The Secret Baby #954
*New Bride in Town #1030
*Waiting at the Altar #1036
*A Good Groom Is Hard To Find #1043
Baby Starts the Wedding March #1188

* Sweet Hope Weddings

AMY FRAZIER

has loved to read, listen to and tell stories from the time she was a very young child. With the support of a loving family, she grew up believing she could accomplish anything she set her mind to. It was with this attitude that she tackled various careers as teacher, librarian, freelance artist, professional storyteller, wife and mother. Above all else, the stories always beckoned. It is with a contented sigh that she settles into the romance field, where she can weave stories in which love conquers all.

Amy now lives with her husband, son and daughter in northwest Georgia, where the kudzu grows high as an elephant's eye. When not writing, she loves reading, music, painting, gardening, bird-watching and the Atlanta Braves.

Dear Reader,

I have been blessed with family.

Surrounded by my parents, my brother and a host of aunts, uncles and cousins, I grew up to develop a strong sense of identity and of roots.

When I married, my husband's diverse clan reinforced the concept that family is the framework within which we learn communication and acceptance.

My husband, my two children and I eventually moved far away from our families, forcing us to create new traditions, to establish a new safe harbor, and to learn that family really is a state of mind.

I am not so naive as to believe that everyone's experience with family has been as traditional or as positive as mine. But I do believe that, regardless of one's past or present circumstances, one can create a sense of family—and I mean family in any of its many nurturing forms—if one keeps an open and a loving heart.

In *Family by the Bunch,* Neesa, who cannot have children, and Hank, who dearly wants children "of his own," learn that biology does not necessarily make a family. They ultimately learn to love, respect and accept "other people's children" as their own. And isn't this a lesson—to see family in the eyes of a stranger—from which all humankind could benefit?

With love,

Amy Frazier

Chapter One

Surrounded by designer-clothed kids and tennis-skirted moms, the cowboy at the elementary school bus stop stood out like a sharply chiseled hunk of granite nestled in a crystal bowl of whipped cream.

Rubbing her eyes as much in reaction to the incongruous sight as against the early-morning glare, Neesa Little reached into her convertible sports coupe's compartment for sun glasses as she waited for the neighborhood children to board the big yellow bus. Remembering she'd left the sun glasses on her kitchen counter, she muttered sharply under her breath while squinting in the direction of the newcomer at the bus stop.

The man wearing the Stetson most certainly didn't blend into the pruned, tamed and manicured landscaping of Holly Mount subdivision. Not a bit. In fact, with his faded chambray work shirt, tight jeans and scuffed cowboy boots, he didn't appear to come from anywhere near Ellis Springs, Georgia. He rather looked as if he'd ridden right out of the wild West. The only things missing were a lariat, a faithful cow pony and a herding dog.

He bent to receive an exuberant farewell hug from the last little girl to board the bus. It was the final day of the school year, and joy showed on the child's face. Witnessing the simple parent-child scene set off an old familiar pain. Neesa winced, mentally chiding herself to quit dwelling on her own biological deficiencies.

As he straightened, the cowboy looked directly at Neesa, whose open convertible idled in the opposite lane facing the bus.

Her breath caught sharply in her throat. Within the few seconds that he held her gaze, she felt vulnerable, wished she hadn't put the ragtop down this morning. Wished too that she had, at least, the scant protection of sun glasses, for his dark eyes seemed to knowingly plumb the depths of her very soul.

Plumb the depths of her very soul.

How silly. The June sun was beginning to addle her brains.

It was just an accidental glance, for goodness sakes. And he was a stranger. An ordinary suburban dad. Probably happily married. With two point five kids, a hefty mortgage and golf clubs in the back of a minivan. The cowboy duds would be purely for macho show.

What special powers could he have to know her deepest vulnerabilities? What interest at all could he have in her? She swallowed hard.

"You're drooling on the steering wheel!" The lilting voice of Claire English, her best friend, neighbor and carpool companion, startled Neesa back into the here and now. "And besides, the bus driver's turned off the blinking red lights. Git, girl."

The bus slowly passed them, going in the opposite direction. As Neesa took her foot off the brake, she glanced at the bus stop one more time. The tennis-skirted moms were hovering about the man in the Stetson like long-legged moths to a flame. Obviously he didn't need yet another admirer.

"Isn't that a picture?" Claire asked merrily. "Do you suppose he'll hightail it back to his ranch come Monday morning, or will the lovely ladies-who-lunch lure him into staying? Turn him into their very own suburban cowboy?"

"He doesn't live here?" Neesa knew Claire would only need one question to get her started.

Her friend inhaled deeply as if she were preparing for the tale she had to tell. Claire English knew *everything* about their subdivision neighbors. And she liked nothing better than to share her observations with Neesa.

"No, he doesn't live here. His name's Hank Whittaker. He's baby-sitting the Russell kids today through Sunday while Evan and Cilla are out of town, working on their marriage."

Turning out of the subdivision onto the state road, Neesa remembered from Claire's past tales that the Russell relationship was rocky. She didn't want to talk about the Russells, however. "Is Mr. Whittaker really a rancher, or were you just guessing?" She had an ulterior motive in asking.

"Oh, he's a rancher, all right. Raises and trains logging horses on a spread off Route 176. A big spread, I hear tell."

Neesa's professional antennae went up, but she tried not to appear too concerned, for Claire would certainly misinterpret her interest in the handsome cowboy. "Well, he doesn't quite fit the nanny type," she offered nonchalantly.

"My, my, if that's not the truth." Claire chortled. "Did you get a look at the fit of his jeans?"

Neesa hadn't. Not really. She'd been lost, instead, in his eyes. Eyes the color of midnight. Intense and probing. With a hint of arrogance. No...not arrogance. Something subtler. More intricate. An aloofness that most probably would coincide with his occupation. Unless she missed her guess, rancher Hank Whittaker was a loner. Someone so sure of the distance between himself and others that he wouldn't shrink from staring into a woman's soul.

She shivered. She didn't like having her soul examined. Pressing her foot to the accelerator, she skillfully maneuvered the car along the winding two-lane. The wind loosened strands of hair from the clasp at the back of her neck. She loved driving her little roadster with the top down, and she loved driving fast. It was a way of easing, for a brief time, the pressure of professional challenges and the ache of personal worries.

With her thumb she rubbed the bare ring finger of her left hand. Force of habit. Why, after a year, should it still pain her that the wedding band was gone?

"Are we in a hurry this morning?" That was Claire's hint to slow down. They played this game every time it was Neesa's turn to drive. Claire liked her gossip quick and breezy, not her commute.

"In fact, we are." Neesa sighed heavily. "I need every extra minute I can squeeze out of today. Unless I come up with a sponsor—and *soon*—for my Kids & Animals program idea, my supervisor's going to make me abandon it. Trouble is, I have to find the sponsor on my own time. Between regular client appointments and paperwork."

"But that idea's a wonderful enrichment program. So many of the kids would benefit from it."

"How I know it. But if I can't find a sponsor, I can't even get a pilot program off the ground. And until I can do that, my idea remains a creative frill."

There were far too few frills in the lives of the kids Neesa dealt with daily. She grimaced. And unfortunately, these particular children experienced far too few of life's necessities, as well. She worked for an unusual private group that helped government agencies find homes—both permanent and temporary—for hard-to-place kids. Kids with emotional problems. Kids with physical problems. Kids who might not ever have a loving home. If she couldn't find them homes, she tried to find support programs to help them cope with life in a state-run institution.

She'd planned her Kids & Animals idea as just such a support program. For the children consistently left behind.

"I'm amazed you haven't already thought of this!" Claire exclaimed.

"What?"

"Our temporary neighbor. *Rancher* Hank Whittaker."

"What about him?"

"Ranch. Animals. Kids." Claire beamed. "Duh!"

"But how to approach him?" Neesa tapped one finger rhythmically on the steering wheel. "I don't know the man. He's not even one of our neighbors. I can't very well walk up to him and ask him for this huge commitment before the introductions are cold."

"Use your imagination. Isn't that what your agency pays you for?" Claire chuckled. "For instance, the pool opens tomorrow. The Russell kids are part fish. Wear your sunblock and play your cards right, and you'll have the weekend to meet Gary Cooper, then convince him to sponsor Kids & Animals. His ranch would be perfect."

Oh, Neesa had already thought of that. But an uneasy feeling made her hesitate before acting upon her thoughts. Heretofore, she'd never held back from a work-related challenge. Never hesitated to approach anyone who might be of help to her kids in need. What held her back now, however, was that long soulful stare she'd received just minutes ago. Something told her that in getting involved with Hank Whittaker—even professionally—she would be getting much more than she'd bargained for.

Lordy, but the suburbs were like an alien planet to him. Even the flower-lined sidewalks, swept and edged and weeded so that they formed a pristine ribbon throughout the neighborhood, seemed too unreal to walk on.

Having extracted himself from the bevy of moms at the bus stop, Hank Whittaker strode down the middle of the street to his cousin Evan Russell's driveway and his own pickup truck. He had a full day's worth of work to get in at his ranch before Casey and Chris Russell got home from school.

A full day's work, that is, if he could concentrate around the image of the beautiful, blue-eyed woman in the tiny red sports car. Sakes alive, but he'd felt drawn to her. Instantly.

Such hogwash.

The only time he'd ever heard a real, living, breathing person tell of love at first sight was when his Pa, Jeb Whittaker, told the tale of the first time he'd seen Miss Lily, newly moved to Oklahoma, with her family at a square dance. Miss Lily had been so homesick for Georgia, and Jeb had been so smitten by the lovely Southern belle, that he'd determined right then and there that he'd be the one to carry her back to the state of her birth. He'd be the one to see her then-sad eyes light up and her beautiful face blossom into a smile. A week after Jeb had met Lily, he'd asked for her hand in marriage. A month later, married, they were settled in Georgia. And until his death, not two months after hers, Jeb Whittaker loved his wife with a blazing intensity. The love at first sight never diminished one iota.

Hank shook his head as he climbed into his truck. Fairy tales.

From experience he knew that far too many relationships—including Jeb and Lily's—ultimately ended in the pain of loss.

Grumpily, he maneuvered his way out of the subdivision. His grumpiness didn't arise from the weekend task at hand. He loved being with the Russell kids. They were part of his extended family. And he certainly didn't mind doing a favor for cousin Evan and his wife Cilla if it meant they could patch up their marriage. But this living in big houses on tiny lots with your neighbors knowing your every move gave him the creeps. He liked his privacy. Even his hundred-acre ranch, with subdivisions increasingly ringing its borders, seemed too small at times. Just maybe he'd be the Whittaker brother to pull up stakes and buy a truly big spread out West.

Out West. The source of all his Pa's tales. The source of the magnificent Whittaker boys' childhood fantasies.

Not more than ten miles down the road from the Holly Mount subdivision, Hank turned his truck onto a dirt road and under a rustic arch hung with a sign that read Whispering Pines. His ranch. His refuge from a too quickly changing world.

Breathing a hearty sigh of relief, he drove between the fenced, rolling pastures toward home. In the distance he heard the soft nicker of his horses. Percherons. Red Suffolks. Draft horses that he bred, raised and trained to be loggers. In the old tradition.

He smiled to himself. Pa had always said that *cowboy* was a state of mind. Hank had carried that concept one step further. It was next to impossible to recreate a Western ranch in the foothills of the Piedmont, amid the tall Georgia pines. But if you believed that ranching was a constantly evolving state of mind, anything became possible.

The sprawling ranch house, ringed with pecan trees, came into view. To the right Tucker, his apprentice, worked an enormous gray Percheron in the paddock. To the left, near the kitchen garden, Willy, his foreman, waved his hat and shouted curses as a very large pot-bellied pig, a plume of red dust in his wake, ran for high ground.

Hank was in for one of Willy's lectures.

Pulling his pickup truck in front of the barn, he waited a minute before getting out. Composed his facial features to eliminate any sign of a grin. Willy hated it when Hank didn't take the feud between the foreman and the pig seriously.

"What the hell you doin' back?" Willy's weather-beaten, toothless face popped up at the driver's side window.

"Heard you needed help with a pig."

Willy squinted and examined Hank's face, most probably looking for any hint of amusement. "One of these days I'm gonna have Reba cook me up some pork chops."

"You won't. Reba loves that pig, and you love Reba."
Reba was Hank's housekeeper and Willy's unrequited love.
Winking at the old man, Hank opened the truck door, then
slid out. "No pig…no Reba."

Willy spat a string of curses under his breath.

"To answer your question," Hank continued, unable to
suppress a smile, "I came back to work the ranch until
Casey and Chris get out of school."

Willy scowled. "No need. That young whippersnapper
Tucker and me, we got it under control."

"I don't doubt it. But I couldn't spend one more minute
than necessary in that cramped subdivision. Not with folks
living right on top of me. Breathing down my neck."

Willy looked down at his boots. Scuffed one toe in the
dust. "Kinda hoped you'd meet a purty woman," he muttered.

An image of the beautiful blonde in the sports car sprang
unbidden to mind. "Now why would you want that?"
Hank asked defensively.

"Tucker and I can handle the logging horses and the
grain fields. Reba's got the house in hand. You need someone to occupy your heart so you stop bringing strays—like
that damned pig—onto this spread. As it is now, it's more
Noah's ark than ranch."

As if on cue, a barn cat with her litter of kittens paraded
across the packed dirt of the barnyard, then wound herself
around Hank's legs. Trying to shake off the image of the
woman at the bus stop, he bent and picked up the ginger
mama. "Are you trying to tell me we don't need a few
good mousers?"

"Mousers are one thing. Vietnamese pot-bellied pigs are
another. And hissy-spitting llamas. And crippled mules.
And half-blind dogs. And mean Canada geese." Willy
threw his arms in the air in obvious exasperation. "And
any other wounded, abused or abandoned animal you can
think to haul back here." He jammed his fists on bony hips,
leaned forward and skewered Hank with a one-eyed Popeye

stare. "Hell, you spend almost as much time on these cast-offs as you spend on your legitimate business."

"Your point?" Hank tried to look stern, but failed as the ginger cat licked the tip of his chin. He respected Willy too much to remind the foreman that he had been one of the "castoffs" Hank had rescued.

"The point, as if you didn't know, is that a man needs something to love, sure. But it should be a woman."

A sudden slice of pain across his heart, Hank gently put the mama cat down in the midst of her mewling kittens. Years ago he thought he had found a woman to love, only to find out she didn't love him enough to live the hard but rewarding life of a rancher's wife.

"Well, you're out of luck," he replied with a forced grin. "I didn't see a woman that so much as even tweaked my curiosity."

Lie.

Willy rolled his eyes. "Well, if you plan to continue sleeping with the dogs, Bowser needs a flea bath. Bad. Like today." He turned in a huff, then stumped across the yard toward the barn, muttering under his breath every step of the way.

Hank shook his head. Willy made it seem as if his boss's single state was some kind of degenerate condition. He yanked his Stetson off and rubbed his forehead. The ranch's Noah's ark aspect, as Willy referred to it, took no time at all. What chewed up the moments was the foreman's infernal and constant confrontations on the topic of women. His insistence that an unmarried state was an unnatural state.

Heading for the ranch house and a ton of paperwork, Hank slapped his hat against his thigh in frustration. It was easy for Willy to comment. He loved Reba. A good-hearted country woman. There weren't many women like her. Women who loved the life Hank lived. Who loved the solitude, the lack of city or suburban lights. Who loved hard physical work. And the animals. Both the purebreds and the strays.

Despite those challenges, Hank had a deep, dark secret that he wouldn't admit to Willy: he *was* ready to settle down. He had a thriving business, his own ranch and money in the bank. He'd love to find that perfect woman, get married and raise a whole passle of energetic kids. A family of his own.

He thought miserably of the delicate blue-eyed suburban beauty in her little red convertible. For the life of him, he couldn't picture her on a ranch.

Feeling uneasy for more than one reason, Neesa rang the Russell doorbell again. This was a pretty sneaky way to get Kids & Animals sponsored. She hugged the warm casserole tightly to her. With this little delivery she hoped merely to extend a neighborly hand…and have Mr. Whittaker admit to being a rancher. She could take the "coincidence" from there.

Normally she'd come right out and say, I heard you were a rancher. I need your help. But a faintly formidable look in this man's eyes told her he wouldn't appreciate her listening to gossip about him or asking for favors—very large favors—before the introductions were cold.

The door opened. At the sight of handsome Hank Whittaker looming above her, Neesa nearly lost her grip on the dish of chicken and dumplings. Oh, my, but the man was twice as imposing up close as he had been from a distance. And even without the Stetson to shadow his eyes, his gaze was dark and penetrating. Riveting her attention and rendering her speechless.

"Yes?" The hint of a smile played at the corner of his sensuous mouth.

"M-Mr. Whittaker…"

"Hank."

"Hank." She inhaled sharply. "I'm Neesa Little from

up the street. I understand you're caring for Carey and Chris for the weekend.''

The hint of a smile developed into a broad, sexy grin. ''Word travels fast.''

''Yes,'' she whispered almost inaudibly, extending the casserole. ''I thought you could use some supper.'' Under his grin and those devilishly dark eyes, she found it hard to concentrate, let alone form a coherent sentence. ''Just being neighborly,'' she added weakly.

''Why, thank you.'' He chuckled, and the sound was even sexier than the sight of the grin. ''Step in and let's see if we can find room.''

''Room?''

He opened the door wider, then stepped aside to allow her to enter the foyer. She always felt a little uncomfortable when she visited her neighbors—except for Claire and Robert who were childless but ''trying.'' These homes were enclaves of kids and more kids and even more kids, and always drove home Neesa's own unmarried, perennially childless state.

Sure enough, from the family room, she could hear the sound of a video game and childish laughter. Too, a delicious mixture of aromas filled the air. Clutching the dish of chicken and dumplings, she felt sheepish. He already had supper under control.

The he in question had headed down the hallway. Trying to concentrate on her mission and not the masculine sway of his broad shoulders and narrow hips, Neesa followed as Hank silently led her into the kitchen where, to her complete amazement, covered dishes filled every inch of counter space.

''Now, let's see if we can find a spot for yours.'' He turned, and she started at the unmistakable twinkle in his eyes. ''This is one neighborly neighborhood.''

So it would appear.

Visualizing a line, a very long line, of well-groomed suburban moms bearing casseroles—winding toward the Russell house, she suddenly laughed out loud.

"My reaction exactly." He reached for the casserole she carried. "Y'all sure do have Chris and Casey's best interests at heart."

Neesa nearly choked on the rising guilt. "What do you plan to do with all this?"

"I'm freezing most of it. That way Cilla won't have to cook for a month."

"Cool, huh?" Eight-year-old Chris entered the kitchen. He grinned. "Hey, Miss Neesa, what did you bring?"

"Chicken and dumplings."

"Hank's favorite." The boy lifted the lid of a dish on the counter and extracted a breaded chicken leg. "Me, I like mine fried."

"Don't you dare take that back in the family room," Hank warned. "Your mama would give me a tongue lashing and more."

"I won't." Chris headed for the back door. "I'm going to eat it on the deck, then I'm going to the basement to dig out our swim stuff. Pool opens tomorrow, remember."

"How could I forget?" Hank didn't look thrilled at the prospect.

"I take it you're not a swimmer?"

"The swimming part's fine. I'm just not keen on doing it in a cement pond."

"Cement pond." Neesa laughed aloud again. "Why, you sound like Jethro—"

"Of the Beverly Hillbillies," he finished for her. "I know. It's a cross I bear." He rolled his eyes dramatically.

She hadn't expected him to be approachable and funny and self-deprecating. No. On the contrary, at the bus stop he'd seemed aloof and stern and very macho. Maybe the difference was in the Stetson. Right now, he wasn't wearing it. And without it, he was still drop-dead gorgeous, but gorgeous in a way that didn't push her away. That made her, instead, want to get to know him better.

A dangerous thought.

His dark hair was straight and a little too long to be manageable. His forehead was broad and intelligent. Under dark brows, even darker eyes took in everything. Didn't miss a trick. Tonight his strong jawline and chin showed the blue of a five-o'clock shadow. Very masculine. Neesa wondered if a heavy beard meant...

Mentally admonishing herself to remember *the point* of this visit, Neesa took a step backward as if standing outside his considerable aura might protect her.

"Hank!" Little six-year-old Casey Russell hurtled into the room. "Nobody will play video games with me! I'm all alone in there. Chris left me. Nobody loves me." In a piping voice, her blue-streak complaint held more drama than substance.

"How awful!" Hank scooped the girl into his arms. "*I* love you. If I ever had a little girl, I'd want her to be just like you."

Casey blushed, clearly enjoying the compliment. Still she affected a pout. "But nobody will play pokey pony with me."

"Did that fact make you lose your manners?"

Casey gave him a perplexed stare.

"We have a guest. Say hey to Miss Neesa."

The child snuggled against Hank's neck. "Miss Neesa isn't a guest. She's our neighbor. She gives real big chocolate bars at Halloween."

Hank raised one dark eyebrow in question.

"True," Neesa replied, chuckling. "My favorite."

"Remind me to come back to the neighborhood for Halloween," he said, his voice low and lazy, his eyes now a seductive shade of dark gray. "I love trick or treat."

She just bet.

He lowered Casey to the floor. With one big hand he ruffled the little girl's hair. "Let me walk Miss Neesa to the door. Then I'll play pokey pony with you. Now scoot."

The man obviously liked kids. That would be perfect in

her professional scheme of things. It was an automatic out, however, in her personal relationships ball game.

When Hank turned to look at Neesa, it was with the same soul-searching gaze he'd sent her this morning. Only in the close confines of the kitchen, it seemed a hundred times more potent. Why did he throw her one of those looks when she was feeling most vulnerable? Her knees suddenly went wobbly. She felt color drain from her cheeks. Felt unexplainably giddy.

"Are you all right?" He reached for her. Encircled her upper arms with a strong grip. "You're looking mighty peaked all of a sudden."

His touch only increased the giddiness.

"I'm fine," she managed, drawing away from him with difficulty. "It's just that it's been a long day at work."

"And here you thought to bring us supper." His eyes turned the color of smoke. Tender. "We're much obliged." Lordy, if he'd been wearing the Stetson, he most certainly would have tipped it.

"You're very welcome." The words stuck in her throat. She prayed her knees would hold. "I'd better be going."

Concern flickering in those dark eyes, he walked her to the door, then opened it for her. "See you at the pool tomorrow?"

"Oh, I don't know." She attempted a smile. "I'm not much for cement ponds, either."

He smiled with enough wattage to blow a fuse. "Well, Miss Neesa. See you at Halloween then. Save me a real big chocolate bar."

He winked and slowly closed the door, leaving Neesa standing on the Russells' front doorstep, weak-kneed, flustered and frustrated. Flustered because she'd just experienced a full-blown case of attraction for a stranger who, for all she knew, had a wife and kids of his own back at the ranch. Kids. It was clear from just a few moments of observing him that he was a natural-born parent. Even if

he were single, his obvious desire for children would eliminate him from her eligible bachelor list.

She was frustrated, too, because she'd paid good money
for that chicken and dumplings at Myra's Diner. Even as
good as it had smelled, it hadn't come close to getting Hank
Whittaker to admit he was a rancher. Hadn't provided the
opportunity for Neesa to innocently say, Is that right?
Funny, but I've been on the lookout for a rancher for my
Kids & Animals program....

She harrumphed softly. Now she had to dig her bathing
suit out of mothballs and visit that cement pond tomorrow.

Chapter Two

"Hank?" Poolside, eight-year-old Chris Russell stopped blowing air into the rubber raft. "Why aren't you married?"

Why wasn't he married?

Funny, but you could hem and haw and evade a similar question from an adult, but a kid deserved an honest answer.

From his lounge chair Hank reached for a soft drink in the cooler. The noises and bustle surrounding the neighborhood pool assailed him. He longed for the quiet of his ranch. But Chris's stare didn't waver, and his question remained unanswered.

"I almost was," Hank replied simply.

"What happened?"

"Oh, she was a city gal, and I was a country boy. We just couldn't agree on most of the things you need to go about your daily business."

"Did you love her?"

"Yup." Now, that was the godshonest truth. And it had hurt like hell when she'd left him. The memory of it still did, at times. The pain provided a good reminder that he might search high and low, but it would take a very special woman to become a rancher's wife.

"I could help you find someone new." Chris grinned. "My teacher's real pretty."

"Have you been talking to Willy?" Hank growled playfully. Reaching for the rubber raft, he ruffled the boy's hair en route. "Here. Let me blow this up for you. Otherwise it'll be dark before you get in the water." He began to blow up the raft, safe from Chris's questions. At least if Chris asked them, he now had an excuse not to answer them.

Casey streaked by with a friend.

Hank lifted his head from the task at hand. "Casey! Slow down, darlin'. The lifeguard will kick us all out, and Chris here hasn't even had a chance to dip his toes in the water." He sighed heavily. Would he survive this suburban weekend?

"Looks like you have your hands full." The voice was soft and sultry and very familiar. But he'd heard so many new voices in the past twenty-four hours.

Peering up from under the brim of his Stetson, Hank saw a shapely silhouette etched against the early-afternoon sun. Shadow obscured the face, however.

"I don't need the raft," Chris said suddenly. He leaned close and whispered in Hank's ear. "She's even prettier than my teacher." Before Hank could answer, the boy dashed off, executing a cannonball in the deep end of the pool.

"This seat taken?" That unmistakably feminine voice again.

"It is now. It's yours." Tipping his hat, Hank gallantly rose from his lounge chair while inwardly bemoaning the loss of his privacy. "Ma'am," he added to give the invitation a distancing formality.

"Neesa. Please."

Oh, *that* voice. Neesa Little of the angel blue eyes and

the tiny red sports car. His suburban weekend just got more complicated.

Having fully expected that he'd never see the woman again, he'd allowed himself to flirt with her—just a little— yesterday evening when she'd come bearing chicken and dumplings. Damned good chicken and dumplings. But now here she stood, intending to occupy the lounge chair right next to him. Perhaps for the rest of the afternoon.

Regrets settled over him like dusk over the mountains, even as his pulse picked up in her presence.

Her beautiful blue eyes were covered with dark sun glasses, but her other attributes, covered only by a short, silky top, were much in evidence. He noticed for the first time that she wore no wedding ring. Trying to swallow, he found his tongue and throat uncommonly parched.

As Hank returned to a sitting position, Neesa lowered a small canvas bag to the pool deck, then spread a towel on the lounge next to his. Kicking off sandals, she perched, ramrod straight, hands folded in her lap, on the very end of her chair. "Well!" Her voice became breathy. Despite the pool paraphernalia, she didn't look as if she came here often.

In fact, with her creamy smooth skin and delicate build, she didn't look as if she was much the outdoors type at all.

The kids in the pool had taken up a raucous Marco Polo chant. Water from a particularly messy belly flop lapped its way along the decking toward their chairs. They both reached out at the same moment to rescue her canvas bag; their hands touched. Hank felt a fool as his heart began to hammer like a schoolboy's.

"Sorry!" they said together, both recoiling.

The trickle of water edged closer.

Again, at the same time, they reached for the bag.

This time Hank gripped her hand firmly, then with his free hand scooped the bag to safety. He grinned. "We've got to stop meeting like this."

She blushed.

Must be the heat, because he'd never considered himself a smooth operator.

To his surprise he found he still held her hand. Within his grasp her fingers were long and slender. Fragile. Her skin was warm and incredibly soft. Never before had he understood his parents' constant hand-holding. Now he did. He could, quite simply, hold Neesa Little's hand from now till Georgians lost their drawl. It felt that good.

Glancing pointedly at their clasped hands, she cleared her throat. Reluctantly he released her.

He wished she weren't wearing those sunglasses. Eyes reflected much of what a person felt deep inside. As long as she kept hers covered, he felt at a disadvantage.

With abrupt businesslike gestures, she unzipped the canvas bag, then withdrew a laptop computer.

"Excuse me?" He couldn't help himself. The hardware looked so out of place amid the trappings of sun worship.

She gave a sheepish little shrug. "I thought I should get out and get some fresh air. But I was right in the middle of something."

"Business or pleasure?"

"Business. But the fulfillment of it gives me pleasure."

He found himself intrigued.

She flipped up the computer screen. "I'm creating Web sites for our hardest-to-place children."

"Whoa!" He held up his hands. *Our hardest-to-place children?* "You're going to have to back up for me."

Slowly removing her sun glasses, she looked long and hard at him. The blue of her unshaded eyes took his breath away.

"Would you really like to hear about it?" she asked. "It's a little complicated."

He was struck then by how vulnerable she looked, even with her hands hovering efficiently above the high-tech keyboard. There was a quality of wistfulness that played about her pretty features. He suddenly felt an unaccountable but overwhelming urge to protect her.

"I really would like to know about the children," he answered, fighting the attraction he felt for her.

"I work for a private agency called Georgia's Waiting Children. We help government agencies find foster homes and adoptive homes for children with special needs."

"Special needs?"

"These aren't your healthy babies typically associated with adoption. These kids are older. They may have physical, mental or emotional disabilities. Or they may be brothers and sisters who want to stay together."

And she worked to help these children. Neesa Little rose in his estimation. "How exactly do you fit into the process?"

"I'm an idea person." She lowered her gaze modestly. "I think of programs to support the kids who may never leave state care. Programs like—" She frowned. Setting her chin resolutely, she looked him in the eyes again. "I try to think of new and innovative ways to make these children who need families visible to the public."

"How?"

"You have to use every tool at your disposal. And lately I've been creating Web sites on the Internet."

Hank shook his head. "I know I'm from a different era, but the Internet?" Computers, to him, meant the games the Russell kids played or the business records he kept at the ranch. Period.

"It's a natural." She beamed, obviously warming to the subject, and in the process, warming the far reaches of Hank's heart. "Anyone with access to a computer and a connection to the Internet can learn about waiting children through color photographs and descriptions."

"But this isn't like casual shopping on-line at a clothing store. These are living, breathing kids." Genuine concern crept into his words. He hoped the hell she saw them as children and not as some product.

"Believe me, we don't treat the process as if it were casual shopping for a child." She looked faintly horrified.

He took comfort in her reaction. "Very often this is the final recourse to finding good homes. After we've explored all other options. Our overriding motivation is our belief that every child deserves a loving home."

"You said some of the kids have special needs."

"Yes, and the Net surfer who is more than merely curious can go beyond instant profiles of the children. At the click of a mouse, they can also learn more about a child's disability or special situation. We provide an extensive reference library." Her eyes widened. "Of course the real identities of the children are well protected. The prospective parents must go through our agency or a government agency before they ever meet the child in person. Our screening process is stringent." There was a fierce, protective pride in her eyes. "Our first concern is always the welfare of the child."

Damn. He'd heard of everything now. The lovely, delicate-looking lady who sat before him was certainly made of stronger stuff than he'd first imagined. And what a coincidence: in a grander sense, she did with children what he did with his Noah's ark animals. Her caring nature made the attraction he felt for her all the more difficult to fight. This weekend was not working out at all as he'd anticipated.

Neesa watched the color of Hank's eyes change from dark midnight blue to a warmer cobalt. He seemed genuinely interested in her job. In the children.

Interested, yes, but when he finally found out about her proposed Kids & Animals program, would he be interested *enough?*

"So what do you do?" she asked brightly. She needed a more solid footing—a little voluntarily shared history—with him before she asked her enormous favor.

A large, colorful beach ball blew out of nowhere and into her lap. Casey Russell came running up, breathless. "Hank! We're playing a game. But we need a very big person to be the goal post."

Hank chuckled. "How flattering! No skills required. Just stand there, dumb as a post."

Casey scooped up the beach ball. "Will you, huh?"

He gently tapped her on the nose. "Will you, *please?*"

"Pretty please, with whipped cream and a cherry on top!" The little girl batted her eyelashes.

"How can I resist?" With a grin to set a heart aflutter, he rose from his lounge chair, laid the Stetson on his towel, took Casey by the hand, then followed her to the shallow end of the pool.

Neesa sighed. Would he ever tell her in his own words that he ran a ranch? She felt awkward now, coming out and explaining that she'd heard it through the grapevine. For some inexplicable reason she felt as if this man wouldn't like prying of any kind, either early or late.

Then, too, maybe Claire's information wasn't accurate. Maybe he wasn't even a rancher.

Maybe she sat here, risking sunstroke and worse—risking letting her hormones run amok—for a very attractive man who couldn't offer her anything professionally and could only offer her the wrong things personally. Goodness, but she didn't even know if he was married. She hadn't noted a wedding ring, but that didn't mean a fig....

In an attempt at self-protection, she again put on her sun glasses. Settling herself comfortably on the lounge chair, she made a show of working at her laptop. In reality she watched Hank Whittaker playing with the children in the pool.

The man was, she had to admit, irresistible. She noticed several of the moms sit up in their poolside chairs, suddenly much more attentive to their kids in the water.

With long, well-muscled arms and legs, big hands and a broad, tanned chest that indicated hard work out-of-doors, Hank Whittaker was a sight to behold. Exuding a patience Neesa couldn't quite believe, he played goal post for the kids' impromptu game. When interest in that particular game seemed to wane, he helped them think up a new game. And another. And yet another. He welcomed all comers. All ages. All skill levels. He refereed fairly and gently, making no child feel inadequate. In the middle of all those kids, he didn't look at all like a lonesome cowboy. He looked, instead, like a man destined to head a large, rambunctious and ever-expanding family.

Maybe he already did.

Unaccountably, Neesa's heart sank.

"Miss Neesa!" Called out in a deep masculine voice, the neighborhood children's name for her startled her. "We're short one player for sharks and minnows."

Glancing in Hank's direction, she raised both hands and shook her head, declining the offer. The children around Hank groaned.

Hank waded through the water to the side of the pool right at the end of her lounge chair. He crossed his arms on the cement edge, lowered his chin to his arms, then looked up at her with a dark and soulful, definitely-hard-to-resist gaze.

"Please." He filled the one word with husky undercurrents, sending little shivers up Neesa's arms. "For the kids."

The man certainly knew which button to push.

"If I recall," she replied, steadfastly holding out, "in sharks and minnows it doesn't matter how many players you have."

"Well...technically." Hank grinned up at her. "But the kids get a kick out of pursuing really big minnows. I was feeling kind of outnumbered."

His eyes twinkled merrily. The man was actually being playful. And far too sexy.

The foundation in Neesa's resolve began to crumble.

He cocked one dark eyebrow. "All work and no play..."

Makes for a nice safe existence, Neesa finished mentally. She shook her head. If she got in that water, if she spent the afternoon horsing around with Hank Whittaker and his gang of neighborhood kids, if she let down her guard, she was in for trouble. Pure emotional trouble. She couldn't afford that.

As Neesa tried to resist, Hank rallied reinforcements. The children he'd been playing with, one by one, swam to his side. Cast baleful glances up at Neesa.

"Miss Neesa," Chris Russell coaxed, "it's always more fun when we can capture an adult."

Her dormant competitive nature awoke. "And who says any one of you could capture me?" She chuckled. "I swam on my college team."

"Ooooh..." Rolling his eyes, Hank started the cheerful taunt. The kids chimed in. "Ooooh..."

In the end, it wasn't the dare that sucked Neesa into the game. It was the realization that she'd come to the pool to get a job done. She'd come there to get to know Hank Whittaker better, so that if and when he finally talked about his ranch, she would feel comfortable broaching the subject of Kids & Animals. She couldn't do that if he remained in the water and she remained on the sidelines.

She rose and removed her silk wrapper. "All right."

"All right!" the kids shouted, clambering out of the water onto the edge of the pool.

Hank remained in the water.

Neesa eyed him suspiciously. "I thought *you*, big minnow, needed reinforcements. You're looking pretty shark-like to me."

"The lady's very quick." He winked at the giggling kids.

"And you better be quick, Miss Neesa," Casey Russell added, "'cause Hank will gobble you up in a minute."

The look he shot her certainly made him appear capable of gobbling her up. But not in the way little Casey meant.

Neesa shivered. "Can we get started? We're freezing up here." Freezing? Maybe not, but she was trembling.

"Yeah!" the kids chorused.

"Anytime you're ready." With a mock-sinister glare, Hank began to circle in the center of the pool, never taking his eyes off his prey. "Dum-dum. Dum-dum. Dum-dum," he chanted in movie-shark challenge.

The kids on the sidelines hopped from foot to foot and tittered nervously.

"Now!" someone whispered loudly, and a dozen little bodies plummeted into the water.

Keeping the mass of children between Hank and her, Neesa dove, stroked and came up effortlessly on the other side of the pool. Climbing out, she noticed that Casey had been right. Hank had single-handedly captured a half dozen kids, turning them automatically into sharklets. The unscathed children flopped like manic fish onto the pool decking next to her.

Now the pool water roiled with the added predators.

Caught up in the fun, Neesa grinned from ear to ear. If only the kids her agency dealt with could have such carefree afternoons. Specifically, she thought of the five Hadaways. She glanced at Hank, king shark, in the center of the frolic. Thoroughly enjoying the kids. He'd help her, she just knew it. He'd help her if she ever got a chance to talk about his ranch.

"Now!" The minnow directive went out.

This time, with six added hungry sharks, crossing the pool would require more skill. This time Neesa dove to the bottom, then, with eyes wide open, maneuvered under the tangle of thrashing arms and legs. She came up on the other side of the pool with only one other uncaught minnow remaining.

"Shark bait! Shark bait!" the swimmers in the pool chanted gleefully as Neesa and the sole minnow child scrambled onto the decking.

With a sharp whistle, Hank gathered his forces around him. Whispered a quick directive. Looked Neesa straight in the eye, and declared, "You're mine."

Oh, my.

She had to remind herself that this was merely a game.

Her cominnow folded under the pressure. With a jubilant

shriek of surrender, the child threw herself into the midst
of the circling sharklets. Piscine hara-kari.

The entire group of noisy kids then swam to the edges
of the pool to watch the climax—the big minnow-big shark
drama—unfold.

Good Lord, he was going to have to catch her. Touch
her. Because she was the last minnow, rules dictated it
wouldn't be enough for him to just touch her. He'd have
to hold her so that she couldn't make it to the other side
of the pool. To asylum. The thought of those strong arms
around her corroded her already-waning sense of safety.
Emotional safety.

It was very difficult to hold on to the thought that she
was here on a *professional* mission.

From the middle of the pool, Hank grinned at her. White
teeth in a tanned and rugged face. A sharky grin if she'd
ever seen one. "Jaws" with sex appeal. His broad shoulder
muscles glistened as he stroked the water. Waiting. His
dark eyes held a challenging glint. The challenge, she
feared, didn't spring solely from the game. His gaze hot
and compelling, he circled. This had suddenly stopped being childish fun.

Oh, it promised to be fun. But very adult fun.

Well, she'd be no pushover. She grinned back at him.
Then dove.

She felt the current next to her as he dove, too. Under-
water, glancing over her shoulder, she saw him right behind
her, reaching out. She felt his hand graze the arch of her
foot. Even knowing he'd have to hold her to claim victory,
she started at his touch. Expelled far too much air. Saw
precious bubbles escape to the surface. It wouldn't be long
before she'd have to surface where it would be less easy
to maneuver.

She kicked. He grinned. For an instant, she got the impression that he toyed with her.

Her heart beat faster. Her lungs began to ache. She was
out of shape. College swim team was a long way off. And

for the past year after the divorce, she'd put fun—boisterous, all-out fun—on the back burner. It showed. She needed to surface.

She broke into the brilliant sunshine and blinked. Took a second to adjust. Wrong move. She felt him slither up the length of her and surface right beside her, his arms encircling her waist. His flesh hot against hers in the cool water.

She had only to admit defeat.

He pulled her gently to him. "You're mine," he breathed in her ear.

He had another think coming.

Because he expected her to surrender, she still had surprise on her side.

Quickly, she expelled all the air in her lungs. Mentally made herself heavy and reed thin. Raised her hands over her head and sank like a slippery eel through his light grasp. As she slid away, her fingertips grazed his rock hard chest, his lean hips, his thighs. She almost regretted pulling away.

Almost.

But the thought of him, just seconds ago, assuming he'd won the prize made her feisty. After Paul, her ex-husband, she'd be no man's trophy ever again. Not even in a kids' game.

With all her might, she kicked, reached out and touched the safety of the pool wall. Her lungs empty and burning, she kicked once more with enough effort to propel her over the side onto the decking. She lay gasping and grinning, her fist raised.

"Power to the minnows!" she declared gleefully before her words dissolved in a fit of coughing.

My, my. Hank watched her from the middle of the pool. For a little bitty thing she had some fight in her. He liked a woman with some gumption.

The kids hooted.

"Another game," Chris Russell demanded. "This time

Miss Neesa should be shark. She's awesome." How fickle fame and favor.

Rising, Neesa reached for her towel. "Not right now." Her smile dazzled. "This minnow needs a break."

"Later?"

"Maybe."

"Hank?" The kids pressed around him.

He'd played enough for the moment. "How do you think this defeated shark feels?" He pulled a face as the children groaned in unison. "Y'all play amongst yourselves. I'll take you on in a little bit. Right now I need something cool to drink."

Right now he wanted to find out more about Neesa Little. A woman with a laptop who'd come to the pool prepared to work, but who'd played—and played hard—instead. A woman with the face of an angel who must seem like a guardian angel to children without homes. A woman who, right from the moment he'd spotted her at the bus stop, seemed to exert some mysterious pull over him.

He hauled himself out of the water and onto the pool edge, mentally noting that he had no intention of starting anything—*anything at all*—with Neesa Little, the suburban beauty. He was just curious. Heck, he'd probably never see the woman again after he retreated to his ranch on Monday. Their worlds were that different.

But right now he was curious.

As he reached for his towel, she smiled up at him from her seat on the lounge chair, and his curiosity felt uncomfortably like attraction.

"So, sharkmeister," she said, her blue eyes dancing, "what are you in the work world? Teacher? Cruise director? Game show host? If so, you're good at what you do."

He rubbed the towel vigorously over his chest and arms. "Rancher."

In a small birdlike gesture, she tilted her face. "In Georgia?" Despite the question, she didn't seem surprised.

"I raise draft horses and train them to be loggers." Without the children about them, he'd gone unaccountably reticent. He didn't want to talk about himself. He wanted to listen to her talk.

"Is your ranch near?"

"Not too far." He didn't want to give out too much information. Not even to an angel with blue eyes. His ranch was his business and his life, not a showpiece. And he was damned protective of his refuge. His solitary life. Damned choosy about the people he allowed beyond the front gate. Even in conversation.

A curious expression passed over her face. She altered the topic slightly. "What brings a rancher to Holly Mount subdivision?"

He sat, uncomfortable now, and scowled out over the pool and the kids frolicking noisily. "Evan Russell's my cousin. I'm watching over his kids so that he and Cilla can...get away for the weekend." He wouldn't discuss Evan and Cilla's marital problems. Blood loyalty.

"Well, you're terrific with kids."

Yeah, he was. He flat-out loved kids. Wished he could raise a whole bunch of his own out at the ranch. His scowl deepened. The problem was that kids were a package deal that came with marriage and happily ever after; in his experience, he hadn't seen too much relationship happily ever after. His Pa had died of a broken heart. His own fiancée had left him, almost at the altar. And now Evan and Cilla's relationship was in serious trouble. Hell, he knew the divorce statistics.

Pain. That's what the flame of passion ended in.

Heck. He might harbor the nesting urge—deep down inside—but he remained realistic. Cautious. He planned to enjoy his cousins and nieces and nephews, for, as much as he loved children, he might have to forgo the pleasures of fatherhood to avoid the pain of commitment. Despite his longing for married family life, he knew the odds of finding the right woman.

A sour outlook if ever there was one. But practical. His

scowl was now so tight he could see the shadows of his own eyebrows.

"I'm sorry if I touched on a sore spot." Neesa's soft voice startled him.

He glanced to his right and discovered her watching him. Great. He needed a pair of cloud-soft eyes prodding him like a horse needed wings. He'd known this weekend was going to be tough; no day at the ranch; taking care of the kids; the normal parenting routine. But the kids had been great. However, the suburban distraction—namely dainty Neesa Little—was doing him in. He wished it were Monday.

Neesa couldn't get over the change in Hank.

Minutes ago he'd been grinning. Relaxed and playful. Flirtatious even. Now he looked liked a thunderstorm rising. What had happened? Had her few questions precipitated this change? The fact that she had a motive for her curiosity made her feel just the tiniest bit guilty.

"It's nothing," he replied, his words a barely controlled growl.

"Perhaps I'd better go."

"No!" The force of that one word hung in the air. "I mean…" He reached in the cooler for two cans of soft drink and seemed to be reaching for an explanation—or composure—as well. "It was just some serious business that came to mind. Don't let it spoil your time in the sun."

He obviously had let it spoil his.

He handed her a soft drink. He didn't smile, but his expression wasn't quite as fearsome as before. "At least let the shark buy the conquering minnow a drink."

He was certainly a complex one, this Mr. Hank Whittaker. Rancher.

Accepting the soft drink, she searched for a new topic of conversation. He wasn't the easiest man to be with, but, with the deadline pressure for Kids & Animals, she needed him. Needed to keep him talking. Just now the subject of kids had, strangely enough, brought on his beetled-brow silence. She racked her brain for some new avenue of conversation. Something that would make her sound casually curious. Not prying.

"I think every girl loves horses at one point or another in her childhood," she began. "I was no different. What's it like to work with them? Especially the big ones. Draft horses that you train to be loggers, didn't you say?"

He seemed to relax. Clearly animals were a safe topic. "Percherons," he said with pride. "And red Suffolks. Real beauties."

"And the logging training…is that for competition?"

"No, ma'am. It's a living. Logging as it was done in the mountains a century ago. It's a highly selective method that minimizes damage to old-growth forests."

What a picture that brought to mind. Rugged Hank Whittaker behind a team of powerful draft horses. In control. Logging the north Georgia mountains. The great outdoors and one great-looking guy, to boot. "Now *that* would be something to see," she said almost to herself.

"I don't give tours," he replied gruffly.

What a conversation stopper. It looked as if Kids & Animals was slipping into the netherworld of terrific yet unrealized ideas.

Saving Neesa the task of thinking up another change of subject, Chris and Casey came scampering up.

Rummaging in the cooler, Chris flashed her a grin. "You're good at sharks and minnows."

"Thanks."

Casey wrapped herself in a towel as big as herself. "You can play with us anyday."

"Yeah," Chris agreed. "Like tomorrow."

Hank scowled.

"I don't think I'll be coming to the pool tomorrow." Neesa could read Hank's admonitory frown loud and clear. For whatever reason, it was becoming obvious that he wouldn't be overjoyed to repeat their meeting. Surely she could dream up a more biddable sponsor by Monday.

"Not at the pool." Casey sidled up to Hank. "We're having a picnic at Hank's ranch tomorrow. Miss Neesa can come too, can't she, Hank?"

Hank looked as stunned as Neesa felt.

"Oh, I...I..." Neesa stammered, conflicting feelings pulling at her.

"Pretty please?" Casey wrapped her arms around Hank's neck.

"Please?" echoed Chris.

Knitting his brows, Hank cleared his throat. "It's up to Miss Neesa." His words sounded gruff as he shot her a pointed look, clearly warning her off.

"Sure," she replied without further thought.

Oh, heck. He wasn't the only one who couldn't resist kids.

Chapter Three

She was in trouble.

Neesa maneuvered her car under the Whispering Pines sign. The bright May sunshine danced shadows over the empty passenger seat. Hank had neither asked for a ride nor offered to give her a ride with Chris and Casey. Heck. Yesterday he'd barely been able to growl out directions to his ranch. She was definitely persona non grata at this picnic. A troublesome addition. As welcome as ants and rain. Here only because of the two little Russells' enthusiasm and persistent pleas. She should know better than to go where she wasn't wanted.

But, having seen Hank Whittaker interact with children, she couldn't resist the opportunity to see his ranch. She had a feeling that if she minded her p's and q's today, she *might* provide her agency's kids with a golden opportunity. *If* she found an opportunity to broach the subject, the Hank who liked children would come through for Kids & Animals. He had to.

Even if he did come through, she was still in trouble.

Emotional trouble.

This had not proved to be her normal weekend. Not at
all. Her normal weekend consisted of trips to the library to
research the latest child advocacy programs, or popcorn and
milk in front of the stereo as she tapped out Web sites on
her laptop. Occasionally Claire and Robert would come by
and drag her out to a movie. But never in the past year had
she spent two days *playing*.

And playing with children.

A tiny, well-disciplined pain tugged at her heart. She
could handle working with the kids at the agency. They
needed her. There simply was no question that she'd help
them. But weekends in the suburbs were tough. Happy children. Happy families. Always reminding her of her inability
to bear children. Always reminding her of Paul's disgust at
that fact. His leaving because of it.

Her need to protect her emotional vulnerability where
children were involved was the reason the big For Sale sign
stood in her front yard. A condo in an urban adult complex
would be a much safer residence, considering her particular
circumstances.

She shook her head to clear her thoughts and concen-
trated on the winding dirt road before her, the property
spreading out on either side.

Such a piece of property.

Rolling pastureland, rimmed with tall pines. The biggest
horses she'd ever seen, grazing contentedly just beyond the
fence. Blue sky. Puffy clouds. Butterflies fluttering just
above the grass. And the sweet smell of the earth. Hank
Whittaker certainly had himself a little slice of heaven.

It wasn't long before Neesa could see a sprawling house
in the distance, a grove of pecan trees arched protectively
about it, a barn not far from the house. This was a very
private little slice of heaven. Her heart did a flip-flop at the
audacity of her intrusion.

Finally pulling her car up close to the front veranda, she
debated turning around and heading right back to Holly
Mount, where she would plug in her laptop and salvage a

normal weekend—Sunday alone and dedicated to work. But then Hank stepped onto the veranda from the interior of the house.

And Neesa found herself unable to move in her seat.

The tall, whipcord-lean man framed in the dark doorway, belonged to another time and place. A time of rugged individualists. A place that bred true grit and free spirits. Even in the veranda's shadows his eyes flashed strength and determination.

Surely a determination to hasten her departure, Neesa thought as, with her own brand of true grit, she opened the car door and set foot on Whittaker land. He might not have extended the invitation, but she'd been given one, nonetheless, and she would make the most of it.

"Any trouble getting that roller skate over the bumps in the lane?" Sauntering down the front steps, he cocked his head at her sports car.

Her pulse performed a tiny riff at the sound of his gravelly voice. Why did she always seem in danger of losing her professional perspective when Hank came around?

Trying to pull her small frame taller, she engineered what she hoped was an enthusiastic and guileless expression on her face, then looked him right in the eyes. "Not at all. I'm an excellent driver. And I love a good adventure."

His dark eyes seemed to go a shade darker. "I just bet."

Well, now. The day was not off to a good start.

Stay on task. Stay on task. Stay on task, she repeated in a mental mantra.

"Where are Chris and Casey?" she asked, discovering to her chagrin that her voice echoed the catch in her heartbeat.

"Helping Reba pack the picnic basket."

"Reba?" His wife. Surely his wife.

"My housekeeper."

"Oh." She hoped her smile hadn't suddenly broadened into a revealing smirk. "What's for lunch?" she added lamely.

One corner of his mouth twitched. "Bubble gum and tortilla chips if Casey and Chris have anything to say about it."

She breathed a little sigh of relief at the lightening of his words. "Do you have time to give me a tour?" She might as well be bold. Nothing ventured, nothing gained. And if she could get him alone, he might be less distracted. She might be able to ask him about Kids & Animals sooner than if the Russell children demanded their attention. At least, that sounded like good motivation.

Who was she trying to fool?

He stiffened. And scowled. Obviously the idea of spending time alone with her didn't strike him as dandy.

"Of course he'll give you a tour." The sandpaper voice came from behind her.

Neesa turned to see a wiry old man surveying the two of them with profound satisfaction.

"I'm Willy. Hank's foreman." He extended his bony hand. "I'll keep Reba and the kids company while you take a little walk. At least show the lady Noah's ark."

"Noah's ark?" Neesa turned to Hank for an explanation, but intercepted, instead, a thunderous expression aimed at Willy.

"Hank'll explain everything." Willy gave the two an impatient push toward the barn. "While you're walkin'."

Abruptly turning his back on Willy, Hank strode at Neesa's side. Silently. With a masculine grace that exuded power. And a simmering hostility. To her dismay, Neesa suddenly realized that this glowering cowboy was going to be a far greater distraction than either of the Russell children could think to be.

How would she ever find an opening to propose Kids & Animals?

Hank focused on the barn. And on the hundred different slow and torturous ways for firing Willy. The meddling old fool. The meddling old *matchmaking* fool. It was Hank's bad luck that he loved the persistent codger.

For a lot of different reasons, Hank didn't want this woman on his ranch. By his side. She didn't belong on any ranch. Not with her elegant blouse and trim slacks and shoes unfit for walking a barnyard. But here she was. Uninvited. Well, Chris and Casey— But anyone would have had sense enough to decline the kids' invitation. Anyone with the sense they were born with.

He glanced sideways at her. A little bitty thing. Why, he bet he could cup her whole head in the palm of one hand. Let that silky blond hair slide over his wrist and arm...

Beetling his brow, he attempted to corral his wayward thoughts.

He needed to be civil to her for the sake of Chris and Casey. At the same time he needed to hasten her departure from Whispering Pines, making it crystal clear that today's tour was *not* to be repeated. His solitary refuge would not be violated again. Especially not by a fragile suburban princess with an impractical sports car that couldn't even haul a decent bale of hay.

"What exactly is this Noah's ark Willy spoke of?" Her voice shimmied over his senses like a warm spring rain.

He made the mistake of looking at her.

Lordy, but her blue-eyed gaze was enough to melt a man's heart.

"It's no Noah's ark," he muttered, trying desperately to rein in this pesky, unwanted attraction he felt for her. "That's just what Willy calls the few animals I've rescued."

"Rescued?" The light in her eyes softened considerably.

"It's no big deal." He didn't want her thinking he was some kind of hero. "They're just animals that have needed a place to heal. Or retire."

"Draft horses?"

"No." The corner of his mouth twitched in a beginning smile despite himself. "Take a look." They'd come to the small, fenced pasture behind the barn. Whistling softly, he pointed to the far corner.

A llama stood watch over three sheep. The beast's big ears twitched like furry antennae. But he didn't move. He had a job to do. Hank had discovered that llamas make terrific sheep herders, protectively regarding their wards as dimwitted distant cousins.

"That's Fancy," Hank said, "and the Three Musketeers."

"You've taken in a llama?" Amusement tinged her words.

Hank put his foot on the bottom rung of the fence, leaned his arms on the top. Looked out over the pasture rather than at Neesa beside him. "And the sheep. And Amos the pig, Bowser the dog, Miss Kitty, several Canada geese, and Gizmo the mule. A regular petting zoo."

Out of the corner of his eye, he could see her place those delicate white hands on the top fence rail, then rest her chin on her hands. "What a wonderful place for children," she said, almost to herself.

"Chris and Casey don't seem to object," he replied brusquely, thinking with regret that cousins, nephews and nieces would be the only children on this ranch if he didn't meet his dream woman. And soon.

He felt her hand, small and warm, on his arm. "How did this get started?"

Against his will, he looked at her and saw admiration in her face. Hell, he didn't want her admiration. He wanted her to go home.

"Look, it was an accident the way it started out. People just dumped unwanted cats and dogs at the head of the lane." He didn't want her thinking he was some softhearted, save-the-animals kind of pushover.

"And?"

"And...I took them in to the animal shelter where they could be adopted."

Neesa smiled, and Hank thought his dried-up heart grew two sizes.

"That doesn't account for the llama." She increased the wattage on the smile. "And the others."

Dazzled, he forgot he was supposed to be merely civil to the woman until she took the hint to vamoose. "When I took the dogs and cats in, I found out that most of them would find a home. But there were other animals at the shelter—novelty pets whose novelty had worn off as they grew beyond the cute stage. Like Amos the Vietnamese pot-bellied pig."

"And Fancy." She squeezed his arm gently.

His mouth felt dry, his tongue too slow. "And Fancy," he repeated dully, wishing to the devil that she'd stop smiling. Would take her hand away from his arm where it felt too good. Far too good.

"And?" She looked up at him as if he were something special. As if he were Noah himself.

"The shelter coordinator knew I had a ranch. Asked if I'd take a few of the animals that needed space. It's that simple." He stepped back from the fence and ran his fingers through his hair just to dislodge her hand from his arm.

"What about the Canada geese?" She looked as if she actually cared.

"Wounded. Some kids with a bow and arrow. Folks knew of the few strays I'd taken in. Brought the geese here." He hadn't spoken so many words to a woman not Reba in he-didn't-know-how-many years. Suddenly he felt self-conscious. The barnyard felt airless. "I think we'd better check on the kids."

"Okay." She cheerfully fell into step at his side. "As long as you promise I can pet the llama later."

If he could help it, there would be no *later*. A quick lunch. Civil but quick. A walk to her car and goodbye. The woman made him uneasy by her mere presence. Her delicate made-for-the-suburbs presence. And her questions and her interest made him very uneasy, too.

Why couldn't his ex-fiancée, Ellen, have shown one-tenth the interest in the ranch and its livestock that Neesa had? Immediately. Damn. During their engagement, Ellen hadn't even liked coming out to the ranch. She'd much preferred that Hank drive her into Atlanta for a fancy dinner and an overpriced show. Wanted him to spend his weekends ferrying her from one mall to the next. It wasn't that he hadn't respected her interests. It was just that he'd thought it might have been nice if she'd shown an interest in his life occasionally. More than just in his bed and in his wallet.

"Hank? Are you all right?"

He started at Neesa's soft voice. Looked down at her china-doll features. And now here stood another unsuitable woman who made his pulse race. She might show an interest in petting a llama, but he bet she'd fall apart in the walk across the pasture.

His thoughts under a black cloud, he headed for the ranch house, hoping against hope Reba had packed a picnic that could be eaten in a hurry.

In confusion, Neesa gazed after Hank's retreating form.

It must be that, for some reason, he'd taken a personal dislike to her. He didn't seem like a naturally crabby man. He liked kids. And animals. And he'd been very friendly at the pool yesterday. But today—on his own turf—he was most definitely out of sorts. Guarded. Shutting down as soon as he opened up.

With a sigh she followed him, cautiously stepping over the barnyard's uneven surface. When she brought her kids out here, she'd have to make sure they all had sturdy shoes. *When.* Ha. *If* was more like it.

She had no time for further reflection.

From around the back of the ranch house came a high-pitched squeal punctuated with curses and peals of laughter. Neesa gaped in amazement as the largest, blackest, most bristly pig she'd ever seen came barreling around the corner of the veranda. In hot pursuit, waving a broom in the air and swearing to beat the band, came Willy, followed by an enormous dog who alternately slavered and barked in a convincing baritone. The Russell kids, whooping with glee, ran after the pig, Willy and the dog. But most bizarre, a pair of Canada geese, their necks extended, half flew, half ran after the lot of them, scolding with indignant hisses and honks. It was difficult to determine who chased whom.

Neesa laughed aloud until the pig veered and bore down upon her, altering the entire crazy parade route in her direction. Something in the charging pig's eyes told Neesa that she would have to be the one to move. She could not, however, lift her feet either to left or right. Rather, she froze, wide-eyed, blood pounding noisily in her ears as the pig rapidly advanced.

Without warning, Hank rushed her from the side, tackling her so effectively that he knocked the wind from her. The pig, Willy, the dog, the children and the geese thundered by as Hank and Neesa tumbled to the dirt, Hank rolling to the bottom, breaking Neesa's fall.

Neesa heard a tiny feminine voice remarkably like her own whisper, "Oh my!" before she found herself lying atop Hank. Stretched the full length of his warm, rock-hard body. Wrapped in his arms. Staring into dark eyes that blazed with intensity.

"W-what was *that* all about?" she managed to stammer.

She thought she saw the glimmer of a grin. "*That* was life on Noah's ark," he replied, sitting and bringing her to a sitting position on his lap.

As with the charging pig, Neesa found herself unable to move. This time, however, a lovely sensuous heat crept over her, clogging her reactions with a honeyed lethargy. This time she didn't want to move.

"You all right?" With a callused finger Hank touched her chin gently, turning her head so that she looked deep into those dark eyes. Any sign of hostility had vanished, replaced by concern.

"I'm fine," she murmured. "Just fine." The crazy thing

was…she *was* fine. Hunky-dory, in fact. Alive and warm
for the first time in months.

In one powerful movement, Hank rose, depositing Neesa
on her feet as if she were no more than a sack of groceries.
"In that case," he said, his voice a low growl that belied
the tenderness in his eyes, "I'd better help the kids corral
Willy and Amos. Otherwise, we'll be having ham sand-
wiches for lunch."

Neesa giggled and wondered immediately where *that*
sound had come from. "I'll help."

"And get those fancy clothes all messed up?" Hank
slapped his thighs, sending up a cloud of dust. "Not on
your life." He turned and walked away with a muttered
"Stay put."

And miss the fun? Like bloody hell.

She stormed after him.

The geese had given up. The chase now consisted of
Amos the pig, Willy, the Russell kids and the dog. It appeared that Willy and the kids were acting together to herd
the pig toward a pen at the side of the barn. Hank moved
quickly to help them. The dog proved the fly in the oint-
ment. His barking and erratic movements seemed to spook
the pig who careened crazily about the barnyard. Considering the pig's size and momentum, Neesa had no desire
to tangle with it.

She could, on the other hand, take out the dog.

Heedless of the clouds of dust and pebbles kicked up in
this crazy game of tag, she danced into the fray. The dog,
she discovered, had no intention of bowing out of the game
voluntarily. Instead, he turned her efforts to capture him
into a new game, prancing just out of her reach, barking
merrily.

Neesa lunged and sideswiped Hank.

"I told you to stay put." His voice rasped in her ear as
he unceremoniously picked her up and deposited her on the
sidelines.

She glared at him. "You need me." Big macho cowboy.

He froze, the most curious expression etched on his face.

"I'll take care of the dog," she continued before he could object.

The pig squealed. Neesa fought the urge to sneeze. The dog continued to whip the ensemble into a frenzy. And Hank gave Neesa's clothes the once-over.

"Suit yourself," he said finally, his words brusque. "But don't expect me to foot your dry-cleaning bill." He set his jaw and returned to the roundup.

Dry-cleaning bill, indeed!

What bit of self-serving fluff did he take her for?

The dog, a stick now clamped firmly in his mouth, bounded toward her, reared up, then planted his dirty forefeet on her shoulders. She could swear he grinned around the stick. He could. He didn't have to worry about laundering the silk blouse. Gingerly removing his paws from her shoulders, she grasped the end of the stick.

"So you want to play fetch." It was as good a way as any to take him out of the action.

He barked loudly in reply, releasing the slobbery trophy.

Neesa hauled back and threw the stick with all her might and tried to ignore the subsequent sound of tearing silk.

"All right, Miss Neesa!" Chris Russell shouted. "Keep playing with Bowser. We almost have Amos penned."

Having turned at the sound of Chris's encouragement, Neesa was unprepared for the return of Bowser, who slammed into her with furry abandon. She felt her ankle twist and the heel of one shoe snap loose. But gamely she bent to retrieve the stick and to throw it once more.

"We did it!" A shout went up from the Russell kids.

Neesa didn't dare look in their direction for fear of losing eye contact with the indefatigable Bowser.

"You're a game lass," came a raspy voice at her side. Willy. "You make a rare decoy," he added with a chuckle. "But I'll take over from here, if you don't mind." He intercepted Bowser. "Heel, you filthy mongrel."

The dog obeyed cheerfully as if Willy had just called him grand champion.

"Come on, kids." The foreman cocked his head toward the house. "Let's wash up before chow."

The kids fell in with the dog, leaving Neesa in a slowly settling cloud of dust, her blouse dirty and ripped, the heel of one shoe broken, her hair falling in her eyes. It seemed that her mission for today had been blown terribly off course.

In the midst of her exasperation, it took a few moments before she realized that Hank stood staring at her.

He ran his hand slowly over his mouth to conceal his grin. My, but she was a picture.

Smudged. And sexy. Rumpled. And sexy. With a flash of fire in those big blue eyes. Sexy. Very, *very* sexy.

He felt a longing deep within him.

She sent him a self-conscious little smile and shrugged. "Noah's ark. I can't wait to load the rhinos."

Willy was right. She was game. And spirited. Far tougher than her pretty looks would let you believe. Far more attractive than she had any right to be. He suddenly wondered what it would be like to see her after today.

Now stop that, he cautioned mentally. Neesa Little had a natural curiosity and enthusiasm. She liked kids and strays. She was here at Chris and Casey's behest. She had not come for him.

Although…he let his thoughts linger on the pleasant possibilities that her interest in him as a man might arouse. *Arouse.* What an applicable word.

He cleared his throat. "Let's get you inside where you can freshen up."

"Thanks." She took one step, her small smile turning to a wince.

"Are you okay?" Protectiveness welled inside him.

Bending, she removed one shoe. "I twisted my ankle. Loosened my heel in the bargain."

"I can fix the heel later." He strode to her side. "Let's take a look at that ankle."

She waved him away. "I'm fine."

She wasn't. He could see her ankle, slightly swollen, beneath the hem of her slacks. If she'd twisted it, she'd probably sprained it. He knelt before her and reached instinctively to feel the affected flesh. She flinched.

He grinned up at her. "Don't fret. I'm a whiz as a horse doctor."

"Some recommendation." She harrumphed softly, but let him check her ankle.

"It seems minor." He rose. "I have an ice pack and some ace bandages in the house. I'll tape it up for you. Then we'll have the picnic on the veranda where you can put your foot up."

"Oh, no," she protested softly, gazing up at him with eyes the blue of summer wildflowers. "I couldn't ruin Chris and Casey's picnic. I'll just go on home."

"No!" Why had he said that? Hadn't he wanted her off this ranch? And as quickly as possible. Now here was the opportunity to be rid of her. For good.

And he wanted her to stay.

"Chris and Casey won't object if I promise to give y'all a hayride tour of the ranch after lunch." Had he really said that? His words, even to his own ears, sounded beyond the strictures of *civil*. He was getting himself in deeper and deeper.

"A hayride." She beamed. "How could I say no?"

He didn't quite know. But he'd been counting on her being the more rational of the two of them. Or allergic to hay. Or uninterested in the simple pleasures of a ranch— the way Ellen had been.

"If you're sure I won't be a hindrance," she said, "I'd love to stay."

"Can you walk to the house?" He didn't mean to sound so brusque, but now that he'd so easily convinced her to stay, he didn't quite know what to do with her.

"Sure." Gamely she took a step. Color flushed her cheeks. The reaction to pain, he imagined.

"Here." He put his arm around her waist. "Lean on me."

She did. And he was unprepared for the emotional jolt he received. Petite as she was, she felt *right* next to him. Fit his side as if she were a hitherto unknown missing piece.

Pushing that unwanted assessment to a far corner of his thoughts, he ignored it. "Take it easy. It's not far." Now he understood Einstein's Theory of Relativity. With Neesa's lithe, warm body pressed against his, the few steps to the veranda seemed a million miles away.

"For a horse doctor, you have a remarkably reassuring bedside manner."

Looking down at her, he saw her eyes sparkle with mischief. He swallowed hard and tried to remember that there wasn't one relationship he knew of personally that hadn't ended in pain or disaster, including his own with Ellen. He wasn't about to give in to tentative thoughts of one with Neesa Little. Ranching and animals and helping out his blood kin were enough of a commitment.

The veranda still seemed a million miles away, and Hank had run out of conversation. Without preamble, he bent and scooped Neesa up in his arms. In response to her astonished look, he muttered, "Time's awastin'. Reba will be starting on supper."

She smiled at him in a way that made him think she might very well be here today because she found him fascinating. Not the ranch. Not the children. Not the animals. *Him.*

Now why did that make his pulse race?

Chris and Casey exploded from the interior of the house. Flew off the veranda. "What happened?"

Yeah, Hank thought ruefully. *What did just happen?*

Curling her hands around Hank's neck, Neesa relaxed utterly in his powerful arms. This was not supposed to happen. This…this feeling of rightness with a man. Any man. This particular kid-loving man.

"Miss Neesa twisted her ankle," Hank replied in a low growl. "I'm going to get ice and a bandage to wrap it. Then I'm going to fix her shoe. You two pull that footstool on the veranda next to the big rocker."

The children rushed to do his bidding as Hank mounted the front steps with Neesa in his arms.

In his arms. That fact made her a little woozy.

The man was all strength and take-charge. Just the kind of man who…*who would be perfect for Kids & Animals,* she reminded herself sternly. After the minor hormonal digression, she snapped her thoughts back into line. Lordy, when the handsome rancher was around, she had trouble staying on task.

Hank lowered her gently into the rocking chair. "Now, do you suppose I can convince you to stay put this time?" His words were rough, but blatant longing shone from his eyes.

Her eyes widening involuntarily, Neesa inhaled sharply. "Yes." The reply came out mouse small.

"We'll take good care of her," Casey volunteered.

Hank smiled down at the girl. "Maybe you could rustle up something soft to put under Miss Neesa's ankle."

"You bet!" Casey dashed down the length of the veranda to a setting of twig chairs with cushions.

Casting one last searing glance in Neesa's direction, Hank entered the house.

My, it suddenly had turned very warm.

"Do you like the ranch?" Chris settled on the floor near the rocker.

"Of course she likes the ranch." Casey, returning with a small cushion, didn't give Neesa a chance to answer. "Who wouldn't like the ranch and Hank."

And Hank. Neesa had to admit it was hard to separate her liking for the ranch from her liking of Hank.

"Then maybe you could buy yourself a ranch like Whispering Pines,'' Chris said, his expression solemn and old beyond his years.

Neesa smiled. ''Now why would I do that?''

'''Cause you have a big For Sale sign in your yard.''

Kneeling, Casey slid the cushion under Neesa's ankle, then folded her elbows on the footstool and placed her chin on her hands. ''How come you want to leave Holly Mount?''

Why did she want to leave Holly Mount? She couldn't tell the Russell children that happy kids like themselves were part of the reason. They weren't to blame. It was her own feeling of inadequacy—her infertility—that compelled her to sell the home in the family neighborhood she'd shared with Paul. So many hopes and dreams gone awry. If only Paul had been the kind of man who would have considered adoption.

But he hadn't been. He'd been a rising corporate star, bent on establishing an executive dynasty in the business world and family blood lines in private. He was not a man to consider ''other people's children.''

''How come, Miss Neesa?'' Casey still stared intently.

Neesa attempted a smile. ''Because a big house takes a great deal of time and effort to maintain. I want to have more time for my work.''

''What do you do?''

''I try to find homes for children who are not as lucky as you. Children who don't have parents.''

Both Chris's and Casey's eyes grew wide, their expressions uneasy as if the thought of parentless children was the most frightening idea in the world.

Neesa had to admit that it was.

''Can you?'' Casey's voice caught. ''Can you find them new parents?''

''Sometimes.'' She was not about to lie. ''But sometimes I have to find neat things for the kids to do while they're waiting for a home?''

''Like what?'' Chris drew even closer.

"Well, I have this idea." She might as well begin by telling someone. "I love animals."

"Me, too!" the children exclaimed in tandem.

"I was thinking if I could find someone with lots of interesting animals—"

"Like Hank!" Casey interrupted enthusiastically.

"Yes. Like Hank." She sighed. Quite frankly, she hadn't expected to find anyone like Hank. "I thought that person might let me bring a few kids from my agency to see the animals. Maybe to help care for them. I know I always feel happier after petting an animal. I'm sure it would make my kids feel happier."

"Oh, it would!" Chris laughed. "It always makes me feel happier when I help Willy chase Amos out of Miss Reba's vegetable garden."

"So that's what we were doing." Neesa touched the ripped blouse seam under her arm. A sacrifice to the cause.

"Have you asked Hank if he'd let you come here?"

Chris's direct question made Neesa wonder why she hadn't stopped right at the bus stop and asked Hank immediately. She should have. And if not then, well, at the pool. When she hadn't asked at the pool, she'd been determined to be forthright at the ranch. But it seemed that she was always in danger of losing professional perspective when she was around Hank. Instead of staying on task today, she'd become distracted initially by the beauty of the ranch. Then Hank's dark presence and his less-than-welcoming expression had fed her inattention. As had the tour of Noah's ark. And Willy, the children and the pig chase....

"No," she admitted reluctantly. "I haven't come right out and asked Hank if he'd help me. Ever since last Friday when my friend told me Hank had a ranch, I've been trying to find the right time to ask him."

Chris looked vaguely troubled. "Is that why you brought us chicken and dumplings?"

"And played with us at the pool?" Casey's lower lip protruded in a slow pout.

"And said yes to the picnic?" Chris inched away. "I thought you liked us."

"I do." Rueing her lack of straightforwardness and the children's disappointment, Neesa sought for words to explain her hesitation. "It's just that what I wanted to ask Hank was an awfully big favor—"

"So you decided to butter me up instead of coming right out and asking."

Neesa turned in her seat at the hard-edged sound of Hank's voice.

He stood in the doorway, a none-too-happy look on his rugged face. "Well, Miss Neesa, I believe you've gone and blown your hopes out of the water." He glanced at Chris and Casey. "I don't like people trying to use my kin. Come to think of it, I don't much cotton to being tooled myself."

Chapter Four

Watching the guilty shadows darken Neesa Little's angel blue eyes, Hank held an ice pack in his hands and felt his jaw muscle twitch in severe irritation. Now why did it bother him that this suburban slip of a woman wasn't interested in him personally but in what he could offer her by way of fulfilling her career goals?

"It's time I explained," she said softly.

"Maybe I don't want to hear it." His words slipped out too gruff by far.

Little Casey's face screwed up in concern. "Are you gonna fight?" she whispered.

Backing up against the veranda railing, her brother, Chris, tried to look brave. As a result of Evan and Cilla Russell's shaky marriage, Chris and Casey had witnessed far too many heated adult arguments in the past few months. No wonder the thick tension between Hank and Neesa pushed their panic buttons.

"No, sugah." Hank reached out to ruffle Casey's hair as he bent to apply the ice pack to Neesa's raised ankle. "We're not going to fight. We're going *to discuss* Miss

Neesa's project." In fact, that was the last thing he wanted
to do. He had a gut feeling that even giving air time to her
project would be the beginning of the invasion of his privacy. If she hadn't been injured, he might just have unceremoniously hustled her off his property, witnesses or no
witnesses.

Adjusting the ice pack, Neesa Little's features relaxed.

But she was injured, and his protective instincts kicked
in. Heck, she had until the ice melted to explain why she'd
deliberately wormed her way onto his ranch. His private
refuge. He would listen, but that didn't mean he had to
promise her anything.

"Miss Neesa needs a place full of animals," Chris began
tentatively.

Remaining silent, Hank cocked one eyebrow as he
caught Neesa's gaze. She'd have to do the talking. He
wasn't about to let her hide behind the childish trust of his
kin.

She cleared her throat delicately. "Some of the children
our agency serves—I'm thinking of a specific family of
five—may never find homes." She paused as if choosing
her words carefully. "Institutionalized living tends to com-
pound the problems they already have. Your Noah's
ark—"

"Now, wait a minute. Just because I take in strays, you
want me to give a home to these kids?" He shook his head.
"I'm a rancher, not a child psychologist. I haven't a clue
as to how to help your family of five."

Smiling, Neesa sat as far forward in her rocker as her
raised and iced ankle would allow. "I think you've over-
estimated the extent of the favor I want."

"She just wants the kids to pet the animals!" Casey
exclaimed.

"What?" He rubbed his neck in confusion. How was
that going to help these troubled kids?

His housekeeper, Reba, came out onto the veranda, car-
rying a large picnic basket. Giving Neesa a quick, frank

appraisal, she wordlessly set about pulling up a table and spreading the lunch.

Neesa eagerly clasped and reclasped her hands in her lap. "I've developed a program I call Kids & Animals." Her words conveyed an unmistakable steamroller enthusiasm. "These kids need the unconditional acceptance animals can provide. They also need to develop a sense of responsibility and accomplishment that will bolster their very low self-esteem. I've read that petting animals and caring for animals provide a wonderful way to add warmth and meaning to such children's lives."

Hank tried not to be swayed by the poignancy of the situation. "I have a ranch to run," he replied brusquely. "I couldn't possibly baby-sit a whole orphanage full of kids."

"Oh, once we got started, you wouldn't have to do a thing other than provide the animals." Neesa had scooted forward until she now balanced acrobatically on the very edges of the rocker and footstool. "And we'd start small at first. I'm thinking of five children, two days a week. I'd come with them to supervise their activities, of course."

She'd come with them?

Neesa Little would be coming to his ranch two days a week! Indefinitely.

Oh, no.

He couldn't afford to find two days' worth of excuses every week to be off the premises while she wove her bouncy magic.

"Sorry," he said. If she could talk him into this, she could probably talk him into anything. And not knowing what she might have in mind in the future, he wasn't about to hand her a blank check, no matter the justness of her cause and the angelic look on her face.

Frankly, it was her angelic look and the corresponding pull it exacted from the region round his heart that scared him.

"Just as well," Reba chimed in. "Kids with trouble usually spell nothing but more trouble."

"Oh, no!" Half rising from her seat, Neesa instantly came to their defense. "The Hadaways may have seen trouble, but they themselves are definitely *not* trouble."

The Hadaways. Lordy. She had to go and give a name to these lost children. If she managed to paint a picture of their faces, he'd be a goner.

"Martin's fifteen..."

Tarnation, but she was doing it.

"Nell's eleven. Thomas is nine. Carlie is seven. And Rebecca is four. The reason we've had trouble placing them is that they've insisted on not being separated. They want to remain a family."

Blood ties. If he understood anything, Hank understood blood ties. He tried to block out the siren's song.

Neesa shook her head sadly. "It's not easy asking someone to accept an instant family of five."

"Of course not," Reba declared, sending a pointed look at Hank. "Folks these days have enough trouble tending to their own without worrying about other people's children," she said with lightly veiled irony.

For a fact, Hank knew that his housekeeper was playing devil's advocate. The woman flat-out loved kids—her own kin and "other people's children," too. He could smell a plot to tweak his conscience and get him involved—if only to make sure Neesa Little visited the ranch two days a week. Although Reba always responded cooly to Willy's baleful glances, she was twice as much a matchmaker as the hired man had tried to be.

"I'll think on it," he said, his tone of voice flat, but his thoughts buzzing sympathetically toward the Hadaway kids in need.

"You will?" Neesa's features fairly glowed as Reba swiftly turned her back and scooted into the house.

"I won't promise any more than that." He wondered what had made him promise even as much. "I'll let you know before you go home." He hoped she'd say she'd be taking her injured ankle home now, thank you very much.

"But she's not going home before our picnic!" Chris crowed, heading for the food spread abundantly on the veranda table.

Neesa glanced at her ankle. "I'm sorry I spoiled your picnic."

"You didn't spoil it, Miss Neesa," Casey declared earnestly. "A picnic can be anywhere." The cherub grinned. "As long as you can eat with your fingers. You want me to bring you some fried chicken?"

"Sure." Neesa's gaze rested tenderly on Casey.

It certainly looked as if his charges had forgiven Neesa for inching into their lives with an ulterior motive. Now, could he?

Sated with Reba's delicious country cooking, Neesa wiped her fingers on a snowy white napkin. If it hadn't been for the chatty Russell children and the housekeeper bustling on and off the veranda, this picnic certainly would have been a silent affair. Hank, now sitting in the sun on the top porch step, his back stiff against a railing post, his Stetson tipped low over his eyes, hadn't spoken more than a half dozen words to her throughout the entire meal. Even though he'd promised to think about her proposition, considering his closed and shuttered attitude, Neesa didn't hold out much hope for a yes answer.

"Who wants dessert?" Reba asked, appearing with an enormous coconut cake.

"We do!" Chris and Casey shouted together.

"Well, take the first slice to your guest."

Neesa could feel Hank's gaze hot upon her as Casey served her cake, then settled companionably on the footstool to enjoy her own portion.

The little girl looked up, frosting rimming her mouth. "So what are you going to do with the Hadaway kids when you bring 'em out here?"

Hank cleared his throat, tipped his hat back on his head and glowered.

"I don't know much about ranches," Neesa admitted, smiling sweetly at the fearsome cowboy. "I'd have to ask Hank's opinion at the beginning...that is, if he decides to participate."

Reba brought Neesa a tall, frosty glass of sweet tea. "Now, don't you go carving up Hank's time before he's even given permission." A crafty wink in Neesa's direction belied the gruffness in the housekeeper's voice. "He's got more important things to do than worry about a ragtag lot of children. Children no kin of his."

Hank shifted uncomfortably on the veranda step.

"Have him take them on a hayride!" Chris seemed to think the pact was a done deal.

Neesa tried to hide her smile. It appeared she'd acquired three allies in her cause.

"Trouble, trouble, trouble." Reba shook her head as she began to clear the picnic remainder. "That's what you get when you come out of your hidey hole into the bright light of day to take on other folks' problems—"

"I'll do it!" Hank barked. "All right?" He skewered all four of them with a threatening regard.

Reba grinned.

"Then let's go on a hayride to celebrate!" Chris exclaimed dancing around Hank in glee. "Right now!"

Earlier Hank had promised to take Neesa on a hayride, but she knew when to push and when to retreat. She'd achieved her objective. She had a sponsor for Kids & Animals. Now she needed to back off and let Hank get used to his decision in private. She suspected he was that kind of a person.

"You three go on the hayride," she offered, pointing to her ankle. "I'll just find my way home."

Hank rose. "First, let me take a look at that."

"Chris. Casey." Reba clucked like a mother hen. "I need help cleaning up."

"Awwww..."

"None of that if you know where your next coconut cake's coming from."

The children, obviously respecting Reba's culinary skills far too much to argue, followed her into the house, leaving Neesa and Hank alone on the porch.

"The ankle's fine," Neesa allowed in a preemptive strike. "The ice worked just fine. Fine. Fine and dandy, in fact."

Hank seemed undeterred by her babbling as he knelt beside her. "Let the horse doc see if it needs wrapping." He reached out and cradled her ankle in large, callused hands.

His touch electrified her. His closeness unnerved her. And his scent—a combination of fresh air and soap—gave her pause for thought about her single state.

"Is it tender?" He looked directly into her eyes.

Yes. His look was tender. Very, very tender.

"N-no." She swallowed hard.

"You have a standard transmission in that little red roller skate of yours?" His midnight blue eyes held a hint—a hint—of good-natured teasing.

"I beg your pardon?" Her flesh felt unnaturally hot where he still held her ankle.

"This is your left foot," he replied, his tone low and husky despite the mundane nature of their conversation. "If your car's a standard shift, you'll need to use the clutch. It might prove uncomfortable. You might want a ride home instead."

"No!" Her voice squeaked. "No, thank you. I'll be fine. As you can see, the swelling's gone." She drew her leg from his touch, then stood quickly to prove her point. There was minor discomfort when she applied her full weight, but she'd have to be on death's door before she'd admit the fact to him and risk the added closeness of a courtesy ride home. "You take Chris and Casey on that hayride," she urged. "I'll be running along now."

Rising to a standing position, he towered over her. "But we haven't even discussed where we go from here."

Where we go from here? The phrase sounded inviting. Intimate.

Was he toying with her? His finely chiseled features were so still and his eyes were so dark in the shadow of the Stetson that she couldn't read any meaning in them. She wondered fleetingly if anyone—any woman—truly knew the real Hank Whittaker.

"I thought it would be better if I left before you could change your mind." She smiled wanly.

He tipped his hat even farther back on his head, fully revealing his strikingly handsome face. "You'll find I'm a man of my word, Miss Little." One corner of his mouth twitched. "Y'all may have ganged up on me, but the decision was my own. I'll stick by it." He cocked an eyebrow. "Now, when do I get to meet the Hadaways?"

"Would Tuesday be all right?"

"Tuesday's fine. You want Noah's ark all spit-polished?"

She breathed a sigh of relief. She was beginning to understand that Hank relaxed when he spoke of animals. She hadn't yet figured out the mixed signals he sent out when he discussed children, however.

"No ribbons and bows, please." She basked in his now easy regard. "A tour and a hayride would be nice for starters." She lowered her eyes. "If you're busy... well...maybe Willy could do the honors."

"Sorry, ma'am." He shook his head and grinned haltingly. He looked boyish. "You signed on with me, and I'm the one you're stuck with."

Neesa inhaled sharply as a feeling of utter attraction washed over her. This man was as changeable as the weather on a Georgia summer's afternoon. And just as heart-stoppingly compelling.

"There are a few release papers you'll need to sign," she said recovering her equilibrium.

"Bring 'em with you Tuesday."

"I...I can't think of anything else." She couldn't. Nothing else besides his intense gaze, his strongly muscled presence and the trace of a smile that still played across his suntanned features.

He reached out and ran his fingers lightly down her upper arm, sending a frisson of pleasure clear to her toes. "Do you own any work clothes?" he asked with a noticeable catch in his voice. "Corporate casual-day dress won't cut it."

Unaccountably she wanted equal time. Wanted to reach out and run her fingers down the faded chambray of his work shirt. To feel the strength of muscle under fabric. Instead, she fisted her hands at her sides. "I believe I can find something suitable," she replied, trying to keep her words cool, crisp and professional.

Under her businesslike facade, however, her senses ran amok. How long had it been since she'd even acknowledged she had senses? Forever, it seemed. And now this cowboy with the weather map moods had awakened her sensual longings in what could only result in a storm front brewing.

Reba poked her head out the doorway. "Willy says he'll take Chris and Casey on a hayride before returning them to Holly Mount." She flashed them a brilliant grin. "That way you could drive Neesa home."

"That won't be necessary," Neesa replied hastily. There wasn't room in her car for the two of them without some degree of touching. And touching was definitely not a good idea.

"Surely you want that ankle to heal properly," the housekeeper persisted. "Otherwise you might have to miss work."

Neesa certainly didn't want to miss work.

"I looked at the ankle, Reba," Hank said, warning in his words. "It looks fine. And if Neesa says it's okay, it's okay. As soon as she turns her car around to prove it, I'll take the kids for their hayride."

"Too late!" Reba beamed. "I see Willy heading across

the pasture with them now.'' She looked like innocence personified. "Must've been a mix-up in communication.''

"Must've been,'' Hank muttered.

"Well, I'll be on my way.'' Neesa walked to the veranda steps, consciously trying to avoid any visible signs of lingering infirmity. "Thank you for a delicious picnic, Reba.'' She turned to hazard a glance at Hank. "And thank you for agreeing to pilot the Kids & Animals program.''

"No problem.'' The shuttered look had returned to his features. Would she ever understand this man?

Silly woman, she admonished herself mentally. You only need to understand him enough to interact with him professionally. Period. No more. No less. Get a grip.

She managed to make her way to her car with no small degree of dignity and physical assurance. Inside the car, she engaged the ignition while Reba and Hank watched in farewell from the veranda. Gingerly pressing the clutch to the floorboard, Neesa shifted into reverse, then glanced over her shoulder to back up.

Her traitorous ankle took that opportunity to declare itself still too weak for a standard transmission.

Her left foot slipped off the pedal, she popped the clutch, and her little roadster ignominiously stalled.

"Lucky Hank didn't go on that hayride after all,'' Reba declared with obvious satisfaction.

Pulling his Stetson low over his eyes, Hank strode stiff-legged down the veranda steps. "I'll drive you home.''

He didn't look happy about it. No, indeed.

In fact, Hank wasn't happy about the prospect of driving Neesa home. But he opened the sports car's door so that she could get out and he could drive. It wasn't the inconvenience. It wasn't even the thought of Reba's infernal matchmaking. No, what frosted Hank was the realization that he liked Miss Neesa Little.

And he hadn't expected to. Not at all.

She smiled angelically up at him, a faint blush coloring

her cheeks, as she moved wordlessly from the driver's side to the passenger's side.

Even though she'd come to him with an ulterior motive, he liked her.

He liked her sunny nature.... Getting into the small convertible, he had to adjust the seat far back until he nearly sat on the trunk. He liked her direct blue gaze.... The seat belt barely fit across his chest. He liked her subtle and sophisticated scent.... Fortunately, the convertible's ragtop was down; otherwise his Stetson would have been crushed. But most of all he liked her because she obviously liked kids.

He liked kids. A lot.

His ex-fiancée Ellen hadn't.

"The steering's very tight," Neesa offered helpfully. "Not at all like a pickup."

He found that out when he meant to make a lazy circle in the front yard and made a tight, quick U-turn instead.

Neesa momentarily clamped her hand on top of his Stetson. "Hold on to your hat!" she exclaimed, her voice a lovely, lilting warning.

Hold on to your *heart,* she should be telling him.

Against his better judgment, he liked her.

As he unevenly shifted gears up the lane, he could hear Reba's hearty laughter echoing through the pecan trees.

"What does your housekeeper find so funny?"

"Me and my womanless state," he muttered, finally getting the hang of maneuvering the roadster.

"I'm afraid I don't understand."

"Willy and Reba have decided I have the nest, I just need the mama bird. I think she somehow sees this roller skate car as a fitting cage."

"Oh, my."

He glanced quickly at her before driving under the Whispering Pines sign and out onto the two-lane. "Don't take it personally."

"Goodness, no. We've barely met."

Now why did he feel disappointment at her rapid agreement?

"Are you looking for a wife?" Her words were soft, but forthright, nonetheless. And wholly unexpected.

Thrown off balance, he tended to be snappish. "Now, why weren't you this frank when you decided back on Friday to ask me a favor?"

"Ouch. I had that coming."

"Neesa..." The feel of her name on his tongue felt somehow intimate. "If we're going to work together, you have to understand that I'm the kind of guy who demands total honesty. Otherwise, I tend to discount a person."

"I understand...and I apologize for getting your attention in a roundabout way." She sighed. "It's only that the kids I work for have so little. Every waking minute I spend plotting ways to make their lives a little easier. A little more meaningful. If only they could experience a fraction of the joy Chris and Casey exhibit...well, I'm afraid I'd use almost any means to hook a sponsor."

She stirred him with her passion for these kids in need, at the same time she put him in his place. She saw him as a sponsor. Nothing more, nothing less. It was silly to even get his hopes up.

But he liked her.

He liked the fight she put up for the underdog. He liked the way color rose to her cheeks and sparkle to her eyes when she talked about "her" kids. He liked the grit and determination that hovered just below her china-doll features.

He felt an involuntary, lopsided grin tug at the corner of his mouth. "You do know that 'any means,' in this case, will have you mucking out stalls, lugging heavy bags of feed, and swatting at flies in the noonday heat."

She chuckled softly.

"What's so funny?"

"Reba should worry if that's the line you use to attract a woman."

Well, now…if suburban Miss Neesa Little hadn't hit the nail smack on the head.

"I like romance as much as the next guy," he said, wondering why he felt compelled to open up to this near stranger. "But any woman I got serious with—professionally or personally—would have to know the reality of my life. I'm a rancher. Ranching's hard work." He squinted with an air of finality into the late-afternoon sun.

"Maybe." She appeared to be thinking earnestly. "But my feminine intuition tells me that a woman who got serious about you—personally—would have to want a big country family. And that's not particularly politically correct in this era of two-career marriages."

Bingo.

Her keen perceptions stunned him into silence.

"I'm right, am I not?" she persisted. "You do want a big family."

He should just keep his mouth shut. He hadn't shared this much with anyone since Ellen. And Ellen hadn't liked what she'd heard. But something about gentle Neesa kept him talking.

"Yes, I want a big family," he replied at last. "Kin—blood ties—have always meant everything to me. That and the land. The two give a man substance."

"Do you come from a big family?"

"Not particularly big. But tight. I have two brothers and a horde of cousins."

"Casey and Chris?"

"Cousins. Second, I think. Or is it once removed?" He chuckled. "My Ma could've recited the family tree like 'the begats' in the Bible. To me they're all just blood."

"Blood," she repeated softly. "You must wonder at me spending so much time and energy on 'other people's children.'"

"I admire you for it. It's not easy for many folk to step outside the pull of biological ties." He shook his head. "Especially hard for men somehow."

"I think it's an ego thing. Heirs. Dynasty. Immortality." She'd developed an edge to her words.

"You must see a lot of that in your work."

"*In my work*...yes."

He puzzled over the new underlying anger in her tone of voice. Up until now anger wasn't an emotion he would have associated with the indefatigable Miss Little. He wondered what experience had pushed her to it.

The entrance sign to Holly Mount subdivision appeared around the bend.

"How are you going to get Willy home after he brings Chris and Casey?" Clearly she wanted to change the subject. "I think I've put a glitch in your program again."

"Not at all." She had, but, the darnedest thing was, he liked it. "Evan and Cilla should be getting back about now. When Willy takes the kids home, I'll hop a ride back to the ranch with him."

"So I won't be seeing you at the cement pond again." The lilt in her voice had returned.

"Probably not. I'm not much for the suburban life."

"Me, either." Was he mistaken or was there a hint of wistfulness in her words?

"Tell me which house is yours. I can't pick it out without the jack-o-lantern and the bowl of Milky Ways on the front stoop."

"There." She pointed. "The one with the For Sale sign in the front yard."

"You're moving?" Somehow that bothered him. He might not be returning anytime soon to suburbia, but he'd counted on being able to imagine Neesa Little here.

"The house is really too big for one." Her tone of voice said she was holding back. "Anyway, I'm not here much. I need to find a place closer to work."

He pulled the car into her driveway, shut off the engine, then turned to look at her. "Your work keep you away?"

"Yes." She smiled a tiny nervous smile. "I guess you could say I'm married to my work."

He supposed it wouldn't be fair to expect a workaholic to find family life on a ranch appealing.

But still he liked her.

And because he liked her, he felt reluctant to end their conversation. To get out of the car. To part company.

"Well..." He searched for continuance. "If you'll be getting a close look at my work, I'll be getting a close look at yours, too."

She brightened. "I always think it's a good idea to broaden one's horizons."

Lordy, but sitting so close to her in this tiny car, he had to agree.

"Thank you," she said, "for the picnic. I had fun."

"You did?" Well, if that wasn't an unexpected bonus.

"Mmm-hmm." She moistened her lips, her small pink tongue appearing and disappearing provocatively. "And thank you for your patience." She bestowed that angelic blue gaze upon him. "I know I disrupted your weekend plans."

She couldn't possibly imagine the full extent of truth to that statement.

"Don't worry," he managed, suddenly wondering how it would feel to kiss her. "Casey and Chris got two playmates for the price of one."

"Well..." She rested her hand on the door handle. "Thank you again for agreeing to participate in the Kids & Animals program. I guess I'll be seeing you Tuesday."

Tuesday? His thoughts went fuzzy as he struggled to think of anything but the gentle sound of her voice, the lush curves of her mouth.

"Shall I drive you to the Russells'?" That mouth bowed into the prettiest smile. Almost mischievous.

Hell. He still sat in her car.

"I think I can make it through this suburban jungle." He felt heat rise up the back of his neck. With difficulty he opened his door, then extricated his long limbs from the cramped interior. "See you Tuesday."

She fluttered her fingers in goodbye, and his heartbeat developed a severe catch.

Pulling his Stetson low, he turned and headed for the Russells' house. Confound it, but this entire weekend hadn't gone as planned. He hadn't planned to meet anyone like Neesa Little. And when he had, he hadn't planned on liking her.

He sure as heck hadn't planned on wanting her.

Chapter Five

On Tuesday, for the second time in three days, Neesa drove up the lane to Whispering Pines ranch, wondering if she might not be making a mistake.

The last time, on Sunday, she'd worried about Hank's reaction to her Kids & Animals proposal. She still had doubts about the strength of his commitment. Added to her worries this time was the reaction—or non-reaction—of the five Hadaway children who sat in varying degrees of sullen silence in the agency van. The four younger children took their cue from Martin, the oldest at fifteen, and he'd developed an uncanny wariness even for a teenager. He was not about to expend any hope or enthusiasm for a project before he saw for himself that it wasn't just an empty hand-out. A bone thrown in his direction out of pity.

Neesa couldn't blame him. As head of this small family, he'd seen disappointment after disappointment. That's why she hoped against hope that she and Hank could create a situation that would bring a degree of meaning to the Hadaway five.

She and Hank.

That pairing presented a problem of a different stripe.

Neesa tried to make herself believe that she could conduct a strictly professional relationship with Hank Whittaker. But wayward thoughts of his body language Sunday afternoon in her driveway after he'd driven her home made her uneasy. Uneasy in a far too pleasurable way. It had seemed at one point as if he'd been going to kiss her. More amazing than that was the probability that she would have let him.

"We aren't gonna have to take care of *those things,* are we?" Nine-year-old Thomas's voice broke into her thoughts.

Neesa looked to where he was pointing over the pasture fence to a pair of enormous draft horses. To an urban child those beasts must look monstrous.

"No," she reassured him with a smile, "you'll be taking care of much smaller cuddly animals like kittens and sheep." She prayed the pot-bellied pig wasn't loose.

"Do they have a dog?" four-year-old Rebecca asked softly.

"Yes. I think his name's Bowser."

"I'm 'fraid of dogs."

Oh, dear. Neesa scrambled for reassurance. "Then until you feel comfortable with him, we'll keep him tied up." She felt uneasy about making decisions so soon without Hank's approval. After all, it was his ranch. But the children's welfare came first.

She pulled the van under the pecan trees, then stopped. "We're here. In fact, I see Mr. Whittaker in the paddock working his horses." What a sight that was—the rangy cowboy putting the giant draft horses through their paces with an economy of movement and a minimum of spoken orders that almost made Neesa believe he was one of the fabled horse whisperers.

"You s'pose he'll like us?" seven-year-old Carlie asked.

"Of course he will," Neesa replied.

"Not enough," Martin muttered.

Neesa didn't have to ask what he meant. She knew that the teenager was warning his siblings that no matter that rancher Hank Whittaker was willing to let the Hadaways pet and care for his animals. He wouldn't care for the children enough to take them in as family. Knowing what Martin meant, Neesa couldn't offer a rebuttal. Her experience had been that most prospective adoptive parents and even most foster parents had their hands full with one new family member. Five at once presented an insurmountable obstacle.

And Hank wasn't even looking to expand his family beyond blood kin.

"Come on," she said, opening the van door and injecting cheer into her words and movements. "Let's see what adventures await us."

Martin gave the younger children a quick nod of his head. "Humor her."

The children got out of the van. Eleven-year-old Nell immediately took the hands of Carlie and Rebecca, the youngest. Thomas swaggered at his older brother's side. None of the children took the initiative and moved to examine their surroundings. It seemed that curiosity was a luxury they had lost.

Hank spotted them, waved, then handed over control of the horses to a young man Neesa hadn't seen before.

"Let's go watch," she urged.

The children followed slowly as she walked to the paddock where Hank waited, his arm resting on the high fence railing. With his Stetson pushed way back on his head, his features were exposed to the sunlight in a unintimidating frankness, his eyes faded to a softer shade of blue. He stood still and let the children come to him as a wise man might let a strange dog become accustomed to a new scent.

"Mr. Whittaker," Neesa said, "I'd like you to meet Martin, Nell, Thomas, Carlie and Rebecca Hadaway. Kids, Mr. Whittaker."

The kids bunched up tighter than the petals of a dandelion bud.

"Howdy." Hank held out his hand first to Martin, then to Thomas. He tipped his hat to the girls.

Neesa felt her heart constrict at the silent, awkward way with which the boys responded to Hank's handshake...at their averted gaze. She wondered if anyone had ever taken the time to teach them—or to model for them—the simple civility of a handshake. She mentally blessed Hank for his forthright welcome.

"If y'all feel comfortable with it, you can call me Hank. Mr. Whittaker makes me feel like my granddaddy."

The children stared at him.

"Well—" Neesa smiled and tried not to gush even though this was no time for awkward silences. "—can we have a tour of Noah's ark?"

"Sure." Hank moved toward the barn along the railing inside the paddock. "Go round through the front door and meet me in the barn. I fed all the animals earlier this morning, but I waited for the kids before turning them out to pasture."

"Where's the dog?" Rebecca asked nervously.

"In town with Willy. Do you like dogs?"

At Hank's direct question, Rebecca hid behind Nell, and Neesa gave a quick shake of her head.

Picking up on the signal, Hank offered a simple reassurance. "We can tie Bowser to the veranda till you feel comfortable with him. Once you've fed him, though, you'll have a friend for life."

Martin slitted his eyes. "That'll be a first," he muttered.

Understanding seemed to light Hank's eyes, and he let the remark slip. "See you inside." He entered the barn by way of a low door to the paddock.

Neesa led the children through the enormous front doorway, then stopped in the fragrant darkness.

"It takes a while for your eyes to adjust." Hank's voice

drifted to them from the dusky interior. A sheep bleated agreement.

"What's that?" Nell asked suspiciously. Of all the children, the oldest girl had shown the absolute least response to this project. Her silence had spoken volumes. And that had troubled Neesa. At least Martin's mutterings were a reaction. She was glad to hear Nell speak now.

"One of the Three Musketeers, if I recall," Neesa replied. "A sheep." She rested her hand lightly on Nell's shoulder. "Come on. Let's go see."

Nell wrinkled her nose, but she did step forward as Neesa headed toward the first pen.

Martin had already jumped beyond the prospect of petting to the savvy recognition of ranch chores. "You expect us to clean this?" He pointed contemptuously to the stall.

"With help at first," Hank replied evenly.

"Who does it now?"

"I do. Willy does. Tucker, too."

Martin shot his chin up in an insolent gesture. "Are they more of your slaves?"

"Martin..." Neesa tried to catch the boy's gaze, but he seemed locked in some kind of macho confrontation with Hank.

Hank, bless him, exhibited remarkable control. "Willy's my foreman. And Tucker out in the paddock's my apprentice. You and Miss Neesa will be my ranch hands two days a week if the work suits you. In the end, it'll be your decision."

The kids all turned to Neesa.

"Is he telling the truth?" Nell asked.

"About it being your decision to help at Whispering Pines?" Neesa regarded the question as a good sign. "Yes. After today, you tell me if you want to return. Then we'll work out a schedule with Hank." She worried that their antisocial behavior might make the cowboy withdraw his sponsorship, however.

Viewing the small knot of children, Hank was struck by

the emotional wall they'd built around themselves. Five against the world.

"Nothing much good can come of standing in muck," the older boy, Martin, mumbled, "caring for a bunch of reject animals."

Hank wondered if Martin saw himself and his ragtag family as rejects, whether his outward animosity was a reflection of inner insecurities. He decided not to bite at any negative bait. Instead he said calmly, "So Miss Neesa's told you how I came to collect Noah's ark."

"Yeah, she told us." Martin avoided eye contact.

The little one—Rebecca—holding tightly to her big sister's hand reached out with a tentative forefinger to touch the muzzle of one of the Three Musketeers. As the sheep wuffled, the girl smiled for a brief moment before resuming a far too old, far too solemn expression. But the smile had lasted just long enough to make Hank believe that Neesa Little's ambitious project just might work.

Might.

With incredible doses of patience and persistence.

The delicate Miss Little's fortitude impressed him, and he ached to help her out.

Sticking her head out of a neighboring stall, Fancy the llama playfully nudged the Stetson off Hank's head and onto the floor.

Only Neesa laughed. The Hadaways stood wide-eyed and serious.

"Step back now," he said scooping his hat off the barn floor. "You're in for a show." He unhooked the llama's pen door, then the sheep's.

No sooner had the Three Musketeers tumbled out of their pen in confusion than Fancy took over, herding them with nudges and soft whistles to the big door at the back of the barn that led out onto the pasture.

"What's it doing?" Thomas murmured.

"Baby-sitting." Hank chuckled. "Fancy's more protective than a grandmama."

"We wouldn't know." Martin declared acidly.

Hank reminded himself to beware these emotional land mines.

Poor Neesa looked distressed, but she kept a positive attitude. "So where's my favorite pig?"

He didn't know how the children would respond to his touch, so he placed his hand on Neesa's shoulder instead. And regretted it. It brought back that feeling of wanting her. "Let's follow Fancy," he said a little too gruffly, trying to remember that this visit was professional from the get-go.

After they'd all walked through the back doorway, Hank closed and latched the half gate. "Y'all are going to have to latch gates behind you to keep the livestock from roaming. Can you remember that?"

"And what if we don't?" Martin asked, his features pure provocation.

"No desserts," Hank replied. "And if I were you, I'd do everything in my power not to miss my housekeeper, Miss Reba's, desserts."

"We get desserts?" Carlie whispered.

Hank winked at her. "What kind of a rancher would I be if I didn't feed my hands?"

The girl jabbed her older sister in the ribs.

Lordy, but these children were standoffish.

Neesa had discovered the pig pen attached to the outside of the barn. "Here's the pigman of Alcatraz."

"Why'd you call him that, Miss Neesa?" Thomas wanted to know. A question. A good sign.

"Because I've seen that he's very good at escaping his pen."

"True?" Thomas turned to Hank.

"True. I'm afraid Amos is uncommonly fond of Miss Reba's kitchen garden."

"You have a garden?" Another question. Asked with real interest. This time by Nell.

"Sure. Would you like to help Miss Reba in it?"

"She wouldn't know," Martin interrupted before his sister could answer. "The only gardening she's ever done is in a paper cup on her windowsill."

"That's a good start, Nell," Hank replied, directing his words to the crestfallen girl. "And I'm sure Miss Reba could use the help."

"What's that?" Thomas asked, pointing across the pasture. "Looks like one of your horses is hurt."

"That's Gizmo. A mule. And he's lame. One job would be to rub liniment on his sore leg."

"I could do that," Thomas asserted. "I think." It was pitiful how his self-confidence wavered.

Hank automatically reached out and ruffled Thomas's hair. The boy let him, but Martin rolled his eyes and snorted contemptuously. It was clear that the teenager would be the one to win over. The others were straining to withhold their interest in this ranch project. It would only take their big brother's approval for them to take the initial step toward trust and participation.

"Well, that's most of the crew y'all would be responsible for," Hank declared, moving toward a tractor hooked to a flatbed loaded with hay. "You'll meet Bowser when Willy comes back from town, and you'll see the geese at the pond. Are you ready for the hayride?"

Not a child moved.

Poor Neesa seemed wound as tightly as a kudzu vine around a rail fence. "Come on," she encouraged, though, gamely climbing up into the hay. "It'll be fun."

The children all looked to Martin, who shrugged in studied boredom. This must have been a positive signal in Hadaway-speak, however, because the four younger children moved quickly to the flatbed.

"Up you go!" Hank gallantly gave Nell a hand up first. "Thomas." He cupped his hands so the boy could get a leg up. "Carlie." Without thinking, he swung the girl high onto the straw bed.

"Me too! Me too!" Rebecca lifted her arms and gifted him with a smile.

He swung her up to join the rest, then turned to Martin. "You want to stand behind me on the tractor?"

Wordlessly Martin brushed by him. With a wiry athleticism, he clambered aboard the flatbed and settled sullenly in the hay.

Neesa shot Hank a sympathetic glance as if acknowledging the enormous task before them. He pitied her. She wanted this program to work so very much.

Hank had his doubts about the endeavor, but a promise was a promise. He climbed to the tractor seat and started the strangest hayride he'd ever conducted. No laughter. No comments. No tickling or sneezing. Only a silence that mystified him. How different from Chris and Casey. Why, after five minutes he always had to caution them to settle down. He would have welcomed some horseplay from the Hadaways. Even so, he gave them the usual, running tour narrative, but aside from Neesa's responses he couldn't tell if the ranch made the slightest impression.

On a rise within sight of the ranch, he pulled up under a spreading oak, Chris and Casey's favorite climbing tree. "Okay, everybody out!"

"Why?" Martin's suspicion proved unrelenting.

"To explore," Hank replied patiently, although he'd never imagined he'd have to encourage kids' curiosity. "Climb the tree. See if you can spot Lost Mountain in the distance. Roll down the hill." He jumped off the tractor. "Pick a bunch of wildflowers for Miss Neesa."

Neesa had already climbed down from the flatbed and was helping the younger children. He was impressed with her caring and her never-say-die attitude. He was drawn to her from-the-inside-out beauty. He saw a strength beneath her surface fragility. There was no denying that she exerted a powerful pull over him, and he was tempted to pick his own bunch of wildflowers to offer her.

He strode toward the big oak, trying to give the children

some space in this unfamiliar environment. From the glower on Martin's face, he intuited that pushing would accomplish nothing.

Neesa joined him as the five children remained huddled close to the flatbed. "It won't be easy," she said in an undertone.

"I've already gathered that."

She smiled up at him. Lordy, but she could spread sunshine all around a man's heart. "I want to tell you that your approach is the right one—a nice mix of friendliness and distance."

"One step forward, two back." He needed to take a big step backward from the attraction he felt for her.

"Something like that." Her smile disappeared. "It's just that these kids have abandoned any and all expectations."

"I don't know that a few animals a couple days a week can give them much of anything."

"When you have nothing, anything is something."

"I think you're wrong." He looked hard at her. "They don't have nothing. They have a strongly defined sense of family. Just look at Martin holding them all together."

"Yes." She exhaled sharply. "Sometimes to the detriment of the individuals in the group."

"You're in favor of splitting them up?"

"Not *in favor,* no. There's no easy decision here… All I'm saying is that I could have placed them each individually in homes. They're bright and healthy and—"

"Together." He reached out to grasp her arm. "They're together. Blood ties. There's nothing stronger. More sustaining."

He suddenly saw pain in her eyes and wondered what he might have said to hurt her. Or to dig up an old hurt. He released her arm.

"It's a moot issue," she said at last, concern creasing her pretty forehead. "As the situation stands, I'd like to take away some of the starkness of institutional living. I'd love to see these kids *play.* Love to see them enjoy the wide-open spaces.'' She glanced toward the tractor and hay-strewn flatbed.

The children had barely moved.

''I think that's asking a bit much today.'' Hank said. ''Let's head back.''

''Are you giving up?''

''Me?'' He smiled, trying to erase the all-out worry washing her features. ''You'll find, Miss Neesa, that I'm as tenacious as a dog with a bone. As Fancy with the Three Musketeers.'' He winked. ''You're not dumping me from this project.''

Closing her eyes for a moment, she sighed heavily. ''Thank you.''

Hank suddenly wondered if her breath was warm and if it would tickle his skin if he held her close. He had to rein in this wanting.

''Come on,'' he offered. ''Maybe we have to show them how to play.''

''I beg your pardon?''

''I have an idea.'' He took her hand and started down the rise toward the children. ''Back to the barn.''

The feel of his hand enveloping hers electrified her. Sent renewed optimism through her as well as a pesky physical pleasure. Here she'd been worrying that he'd seen enough of the Hadaways' reluctance and would bail out of the project. But he hadn't. Furthermore, he seemed intuitively to understand not only the obstacles but also, in a way, the children's perspective. She was the coordinator of this project, but here he was, brainstorming with an amazing flexibility as they picked their way through an emotional minefield. He was quite a man, Hank Whittaker.

But what could he be planning back at the barn?

She squeezed his hand in a gesture of appreciation. When he squeezed back, appreciation turned to a lovely nameless glow. She had to remind herself that this was a *professional* relationship.

The two adults rounded up the children for a second

silent trip, this time back to the barnyard. The only comment came when Thomas spied one of the big draft horses rolling on his back in the dusty paddock. "What's he doing?"

"He might be scratching an itch," Hank replied. "Or he might be trying to tell Tucker he's had enough of lessons for today. Or he might just be having some fun."

"Fun." Martin spoke the word as if it were poison.

"Sure." Hank stopped the tractor near the barn. "Maybe I misled you. Not everything on the ranch is about work. I'll show you."

"What now?" Nell asked, but she asked it with the tiniest hint of enthusiasm.

"Well, you won't see, sitting in the hay like a bunch of nesting chickens," Hank called out over his shoulder as he disappeared around the corner of the barn. My, but his grin was boyish. And infectious.

Neesa helped the little ones off the flatbed, then called out, "Last one there's a rotten egg."

Rebecca, Carlie and Thomas scampered after Hank. Nell hung back with Martin, who muttered, "Watch where you step. There's more than rotten eggs in this barnyard."

"Why, Martin!" Neesa exclaimed. "Was that a joke?"

The teenager merely rolled his eyes.

When the three turned the corner, what a sight met them. Hank stood, arms upraised on the top of a very tall haystack. "King of the mountain!" he shouted as the three youngest children stared up at him open-mouthed.

"Oh, no you're not!" Neesa hooted, her natural born competition kicking in. "Come on, kids, let's get him!"

Assaulting the haystack, she found the ascent slippery and difficult. Dust wafted up her nose. Her short-sleeved T-shirt made it possible for the hay to tickle the delicate underside of her arms. She sneezed as Hank taunted her from above.

"So the minnow finds it harder swimming upstream."

She paused long enough to look up and see blatant mischief in his dark eyes and the same sexy grin he'd worn in the subdivision pool. Well, she was game.

The only difference here was the reaction of the children. The Hadaways weren't your usual self-assured suburban kids. They stuck together, watching in wide-eyed wonder. Occasionally a tentative smile would skim across a mouth. Occasionally. But it disappeared almost before it began. Perhaps Hank had been right. Perhaps he and she needed to show them how to play.

Laughing, she clawed her way up the haystack. When she reached the top, Hank eluded her by dropping to his seat and sliding, neat as you please down the sloped hay to land right at the Hadaways' feet. Rebecca actually shrieked with glee.

Hank looked right at her. "You want to try it, sugah?"

"Yes!" Rebecca couldn't have been more emphatic.

"She might get hurt," Martin cautioned.

"Not if Miss Neesa guides her up top and I catch her at the bottom," Hank replied. "Okay?"

"Okay," Martin agreed grudgingly.

Neesa silently praised Hank for asking permission.

Hank took Rebecca's hand, then looked up at Neesa. "Ready?"

Neesa almost forgot to answer, so breathtakingly beautiful did Hank look with a child at his side. He would make one heck of a father when he finally decided to settle down and have a family of his own.

"Ready, Miss Neesa?" Rebecca seemed eager to start.

"You bet!"

Hank helped the little girl climb the haystack. As he handed her off to Neesa, his hand touched hers, and once again, Neesa was struck by his strength underlaid with gentleness. A woman could fall for him...unless the woman were absolutely wrong for him.

She hastily drew her thoughts back to Rebecca's welfare. Scarcely had Hank repositioned himself at the foot of the haystack than Rebecca plopped down on her fanny and slid into his waiting arms.

"I want to try it!" Thomas didn't wait for help climbing the stack. He was at the top almost before Hank had put Rebecca back on her feet.

"Me, too!" Carlie flew after her brother.

Within minutes the three youngest Hadaways were playing and laughing as if they'd lived on this ranch all their lives.

"I'll have to have Willy help me put up a swing in the barn," Hank said offhandedly.

"Really?" Carlie seemed not to believe the good luck.

"Really," Hank promised, and Neesa felt an overwhelming attraction for this big-hearted man.

Only Nell and Martin didn't join in the fun. But Nell's body language said she'd relaxed, if only slightly. Every once in a while the antics of her younger siblings coaxed a wan smile from her. The smile was worth the rash Neesa knew she was sure to develop from her new jeans and an unquantifiable amount of hay dust.

Martin on the other hand remained rigid.

Neesa stayed on the top of the haystack, and Hank stood at the bottom, spotting the children in their romp until the dinner bell and Reba's voice could be heard from the veranda. "Y'all going to play the day away, or are you up for some serious eating?" she shouted.

"Just once more," Rebecca pleaded.

She, Carlie and Thomas each took one more turn at climbing and sliding, then ran to hug Nell who brushed them off and clucked over them like a mother hen.

"I'll show you where we wash up," Hank said, "after I convince Miss Queen of the Mountain here that recess is over." He grinned up at Neesa.

The utter joy of the moment took over. The sunshine, Hank's generosity, and the reaction of the three youngest Hadaways to simple country fun made Neesa feel carefree and girlish.

"Catch me!" she cried, spontaneously dropping to her bottom and sliding down the slippery hay stack. "You couldn't in the pool!"

She skidded to a halt at Hank's feet. She heard him laugh. Felt his hands around her waist. Looked up in the dazzling sunlight to find him looking down at her with unmistakable desire written in his eyes. He pulled her close, so close little puffs of dust rose in the heated afternoon air where their two bodies had come together. She reached out to touch his cheek...

And remembered the children.

Stepping out of Hank's embrace, she looked at the Hadaways. Rebecca giggled. Carlie and Thomas grinned. Nell blushed. And Martin glowered as if he'd seen the devil himself.

While Neesa and Reba were loading the Hadaways into the van for the return trip to the state home, Hank went back into the ranch kitchen to retrieve his Stetson. He shook his head to think of the children packing away his housekeeper's cooking earlier. They might not be able to play easily, but they had no trouble eating. His heart ached as he'd watched them wolf down the meal as if they might not see another. At first appearance they looked reasonably well fed, so he figured it must be a psychological need, some perceived void they tried to fill.

He now entered the kitchen only to see Martin stuffing his pockets with Reba's leftover biscuits. Hank's initial reaction was to lecture the boy on not taking what wasn't his. But the look on Martin's face stayed his words.

No furtiveness lurked about the teenager's features. Instead, the light in his eyes, the set of his chin, the thrust of his shoulders told of a steely determination.

"Martin," Hank asked softly, "what are you doing?"

Martin didn't answer.

"You may have all the biscuits you want. You'll flatter

Reba to where there'll be no living with her.'' Hank paused. ''I only want you to ask.''

''They're not for me.''

''Then who?''

''The little ones get hungry between meals.''

Hank remembered how his Ma had labeled his two brothers and him a horde of locusts for their nonstop forays into the pantry. He didn't think there would be many opportunities for the Hadaways to raid the refrigerator in the institution.

''Plus,'' Martin added, ''I never want to take our next meal for granted.''

Our next meal. He was taking the biscuits in an attempt to provide for his siblings. His family. Blood loyalty. Protection. And pride.

''I can understand that,'' Hank replied simply. He could. Oh, how he could. And because of this connection, he would try to help the Hadaways.

''You can?''

''Yes.''

A silence descended upon the room as the boy took the man's measure.

''Can I take the biscuits?'' Martin asked at last.

''Yes.'' Hank pulled a plastic food-storage bag out of a drawer, then handed it to the boy.

As Martin transferred the biscuits to the bag, he seemed to study the process intently. ''Why did you agree to let us come to your ranch?'' His words a raspy whisper, he didn't look up.

''Miss Neesa thought you might find my ranch interesting.''

''Miss Neesa your girlfriend?'' Martin suddenly made eye contact.

''No,'' Hank replied, wanting to add *not yet*.

''Good,'' the boy growled, turning quickly to leave the kitchen.

Chapter Six

"What have you gotten yourself into now?" county sheriff Brett Whittaker asked as he sprawled in a rocker on his younger brother, Hank's, veranda. The early evening hum of cicadas had begun in earnest. Brett scowled at Hank as if the noise bored a hole in his head.

"You're making a mountain out of a molehill," Hank replied. Lately Brett had gone beyond his usual gruff nature. He was downright irascible. Hank hadn't yet figured out why, and Brett hadn't taken the time to explain.

"Once Neesa Little gets this program off the ground," Hank explained patiently, "I'll have nothing to do with Kids & Animals. I've simply donated the site and the animals necessary for her to do her thing."

Brett snorted his disagreement.

"What?"

"Noah's ark all over again. Only this time it's with kids."

"I don't remember asking your permission to participate in the program." From his seat in a rocker Hank thunked his boot heels up on the porch railing. "All I asked for was a little professional advice concerning a fifteen-year-old boy.''

''What makes you think I have the answers when it comes to other people's kids?''

''Because you regularly work with youngsters in your juvenile programs.'' Hank was beginning to lose patience.

''That doesn't mean I've found all the answers.''

''Lordy, but you've gotten cynical.'' Hank swung, punching his brother's arm. Hard. ''Just tell me if it's possible this boy has a crush on the woman running the program. If he could see me as some kind of rival.''

''Maybe.'' Staring straight out into the front yard, Brett pulled his Stetson low over his eyes. ''Or maybe he thinks if you and this Miss Little are an item, you may become serious. May marry. May start a family of your own. May decide this Kids & Animals thing is too much trouble. Then where would the Hadaway kids be?''

''Geez Louise, the kid would think that far ahead?''

''If he's smart. And if he's as protective of his siblings as you say he is.''

''He is.''

''Tell me one thing.'' Lifting his Stetson, Brett leaned forward and looked Hank right in the eye. ''Are you sweet on this Neesa Little?''

Hank didn't feel like parading his emerging feelings for Neesa out in the open under Brett's hard-hearted scrutiny. ''No.''

''Then why are you sticking your neck out for other people's kids when what you really need is a wife and a family of your own?''

It was Hank's turn to scowl at the empty barnyard. ''You been talking to Willy and Reba?''

''I don't have to. I can smell the nesting urge on you.''

''That's manure. Willy left me cleaning out stalls alone today.''

''Smells more like clean clothes and aftershave to me.'' Brett chuckled. A rusty sound that faded quickly. ''A word of advice, all the same. If you insist on getting involved with problem kids, don't set your expectations too high.''

''You know, I think I can smell hard and crusty sheriff all over you. Maybe it's time for a career change?''

Brett crossed his arms tightly over his chest. ''I just got elected.''

''Then why the burned-out attitude?''

''I've got a lot on my mind, little brother. First I have to clean up the department I inherited. Then I need to get a good PR campaign started....''

Hank barely heard his brother's explanation, for his concentration was focused on a red sports car convertible coming up the lane.

Neesa Little's.

The Hadaway children had decided they wanted to try the Kids & Animals program at Whispering Pines after all, and Neesa had suggested that she and Hank get together to work a few things out before she brought the five back on Friday.

They'd made an appointment for Wednesday night. Tonight.

He couldn't wait.

''...and then I thought I'd join the next circus that rolls through town.''

''Uh-huh,'' Hank agreed.

''That does it.'' Brett stood up. ''I'm not leaving till I meet her.''

''Who?''

''The woman who's got you drooling all over your front porch.''

Swallowing hard, Hank stood up also. ''You're not the only one who's got a lot on his mind. I do, too.'' He stared at Brett pointedly. ''Ranch business.''

''Monkey business,'' Brett muttered under his breath as Neesa pulled to a stop at the bottom of the steps.

''Cut it out,'' Hank muttered right back, jabbing Brett in

the ribs, remembering how the Whittaker boys used to find themselves wrestling in the dust over less.

Neesa emerged from the car, and Hank couldn't stop the grin that spread across his face.

"Hank," she said in greeting as she mounted the steps. "Sheriff Whittaker."

Brett removed his Stetson. "I believe you have me at a disadvantage."

Hank flinched at Brett's practiced smoothness. Of the three Whittaker boys, Brett, although the most hardened, was the most popular with the ladies. The playboy of Cates County. Ladies man or not, he had no right practicing *anything* on Neesa Little.

Hank stepped protectively toward her.

Neesa extended her hand to Brett. "Neesa Little. I work with Georgia's Waiting Children."

"And now, I hear, with my brother Hank."

Neesa looked from one to the other. "I should have realized it earlier. Family's written all over your face."

"Well, graffiti'll be written all over the new middle school if I don't get back to my patrol." Brett gave Neesa one of his killer grins, and Hank could have smacked him. "See you two around."

Brett descended the steps, then paused before getting into his patrol car. "Hank. If you decide to forgo that *business* you were contemplating, I might give it a try."

Subtle, Hank thought wryly. *Real subtle, Brett. Like I'd even let you near Neesa Little. Brother or no.*

He put his hand lightly but possessively on Neesa's back as he glowered at Brett's retreating form. "Shall we sit out here or go inside where there's a table?"

Neesa cocked her head and looked up at Hank. She didn't quite know what had just transpired here. She thought it wise, however, not to press the issue.

"Will we be in Reba's way inside?" she asked instead.

"Reba's gone home for the night."

"Willy?"

"At the movies."

"Tucker?"

"Called it a day, too." Relaxing visibly, he grinned at her. The same grin he'd given her in the pool and from the top of the haystack. "It's just you and me."

Oh, my.

"Let's stay outside," she decided quickly.

"Okay." There was a warmth in his eyes she'd never seen before. "The view from the porch is a corker, I admit," he added, "but I can do it one better. Follow me."

This clearly did not fit the definition of a professional meeting, but Neesa followed him, anyway. How could she not? The evening air, filled with the scent of honeysuckle, was soft and most unprofessional. The light was dusky and languid, not at all conducive to formal business. And a whippoorwill had started its plaintive call. A lonely call.

It was far better to be with someone you liked.

And Neesa had long ago given up her struggle not to admit that she liked Hank Whittaker.

He led her across the barnyard to the paddock fence. "Up you go."

"I beg your pardon?"

"You have to sit on the top rail if you're going to get the best view of the moonrise." He wasn't wearing his Stetson. His eyes were a clear and deep blue in the fading light. His expression softer than she'd ever seen it. More accessible. More inviting.

But what invitation was he extending?

"Hank, I really came to discuss Kids & Animals."

"We will. Talking business and watching the moonrise isn't half as hard as patting your head and rubbing your stomach at the same time."

He'd caught her off guard, and she smiled. And accepted his outstretched hand.

As he helped her climb to the top rail, she wondered how many times had he touched her in their short acquaintance? Numerous times. And at no time could she have construed his touch as coming on to her. But there was an intimacy nonetheless. An intimacy not at all unwanted.

Settling next to her, he pointed to a stand of pines beyond the paddock now bathed in purple shadow. A silvery glow lit the skeletal tree branches, but the moon hadn't yet risen. "Over there. In about fifteen minutes," he said.

Feeling the unmistakable warmth of his body next to hers, she inhaled sharply. "About the Hadaways…any questions so far?" She *must* stay focused.

"One." His voice was mellow. Deep and relaxed. "On Tuesday I caught Martin filling his pockets with leftover biscuits."

"What did you do about it?"

"We talked. He said the younger kids sometimes get hungry between meals. Said, too, that he wanted a little insurance against the prospect of their next meal."

"His survival instincts are sharply honed."

Hank clasped his hands and leaned forward on his thighs. "More than that, I was impressed with his commitment to his kin."

"What's your question?"

"In this experiment of yours, you're not going to move these kids around, maybe to another farm or ranch, once we get started at Whispering Pines, are you?"

"No. Not unless you take away your sponsorship."

"I wouldn't do that," he replied, his voice gruff. "It really wrenched my insides watching this kid try to provide a shred of stability for his brother and sisters. If they can find a little bit more by coming to my ranch on Tuesdays and Fridays, well, I want to give them that, too."

"Oh, Hank…" Neesa examined his chiseled profile in the intensifying moonlight. Such a big strong man he was. With a soft spot in his heart to make a woman go all mushy. "Thank you."

"You know, my first instinct was to lecture the kid for taking what wasn't his, but I'm glad I didn't act on instinct. I would have missed the point." He glanced in her direction. "I admire the stand-up man in Martin. His protective reflexes. As I said before, the Whittakers are a tight bunch. And if I ever have my own children, I hope I can instill in them a true sense of loyalty toward each other. In good times and in bad."

"You really want children of your own." It was an observation, not a question.

"I think most men do if you can get 'em to admit it." He ran his fingers through his hair in a self-conscious gesture. "I guess I'd like to see if I couldn't straighten out some of my own faults with a new generation."

"What else?" She needed to see how deep his sentiment ran.

"I'd like to pass this land on to a Whittaker."

"And?"

"Heck." He looked full at her with mischief written all over his handsome features. "My aunt tells me I was one cute kid. Trouble was, I was too busy being a kid at the time to take notice. Maybe I just want to see how cute I was in the faces of my own young 'uns."

"What about adoption?" He could tell her it was none of her business, but she just had to know. "Have you ever considered it?"

He rubbed his chin thoughtfully. "Nope. Never saw much need." He grinned. "Whittaker men have always been potent varmints."

"I heard cowboys had big egos." She swatted his arm playfully, but her heart sank. Here was a man who truly wanted *his own* family, a biological dynasty…and she could never help him fulfill that dream.

Despite the undeniable attraction she felt for him, she would guard her heart carefully and stick to business, even though the biggest, most romantic moon she'd ever seen had just topped the pines.

"So Tuesdays and Fridays will be good for you?" she asked with as much equanimity as she could muster.

"Sure. Do you think we'll need any time outside of

that—just the two of us—to discuss how things are progressing?"

When she'd arrived this evening, she'd planned to propose just that. But now that she was in his presence it became clear once again that she needed to keep her emotions safe from Hank Whittaker. The less time spent alone together the better.

"I could call you," she offered weakly.

"It'd be better if you stopped by. That way if Reba, Willy or Tucker had any concerns, we could all discuss them."

Oh, great. He had to turn out to be attractive *and* logical.

"*If* we have anything to discuss out of earshot of the kids...or maybe paperwork...I could call, then stop over for a few minutes. On an as-needed basis."

"As needed. Sure."

She wouldn't look at him, but felt certain she heard a smile in his words. "So what'll we have the kids do on Friday?"

"They might as well roll up their sleeves and begin taking care of the animals. I'll help you at first. Later I won't wander too far if you need me." He shifted his weight toward her. "Well now, would you look at that moon."

No. She couldn't risk looking at it one minute longer. Not with Hank Whittaker at her side. She turned carefully on her perch, then hopped to the ground. "I have some release forms in my car for you to sign."

He seemed reluctant to get back to business. "Can I offer you some sweet tea? Reba makes the best."

"No, thank you." She brushed imaginary dust off her jeans. Funny how she'd automatically changed into jeans and a T-shirt before she'd driven out here. As if this was in some way not exactly a professional call.

Hank slowly lowered himself to stand beside her. "I see you turned in your corporate-fancy clothes." He reached out and ran a finger under the hem of her T-shirt sleeve,

The Silhouette Reader Service® — Here's how it works:

Accepting your 2 free books and mystery gift places you under no obligation to buy anything. You may keep the books and gift and return the shipping statement marked "cancel." If you do not cancel, about a month later we'll send you 6 additional novels and bill you just $2.90 each in the U.S.; or $3.25 in Canada, plus 25¢ delivery per book and applicable taxes if any.* That's the complete price and — compared to the cover price of $3.50 in the U.S. and $3.99 in Canada — it's quite a bargain! You may cancel at any time, but if you choose to continue, every month we'll send you 6 more books, which you may either purchase at the discount price or return to us and cancel your subscription.

*Terms and prices subject to change without notice. Sales tax applicable in N.Y. Canadian residents will be charged applicable provincial taxes and GST.

NO POSTAGE
NECESSARY
IF MAILED
IN THE
UNITED STATES

BUSINESS REPLY MAIL

FIRST-CLASS MAIL   PERMIT NO. 717   BUFFALO, NY

POSTAGE WILL BE PAID BY ADDRESSEE

SILHOUETTE READER SERVICE
3010 WALDEN AVE
PO BOX 1867
BUFFALO NY 14240-9952

If offer card is missing write to: Silhouette Reader Service, 3010 Walden Ave., P.O. Box 1867, Buffalo NY 14240-1867

Play The *Lucky Hearts* Game

and get... FREE BOOKS, a FREE GIFT... and MUCH more!

yes! I have scratched off the silver card. Please send me my **2 FREE BOOKS** and **FREE MYSTERY GIFT**. I understand that I am under no obligation to purchase any books as explained on the back of this card.

Scratch Here!
then look below to see what your cards get you...

315 SDL CNGD   **215 SDL CNGC**

Name
(PLEASE PRINT)

Address   Apt.#

City   State/Prov.   Zip/Postal Code

Twenty-one gets you **2 FREE BOOKS** and a **FREE MYSTERY GIFT!**

Twenty gets you **2 FREE BOOKS!**

Nineteen gets you **1 FREE BOOK!**

TRY AGAIN!

Offer limited to one per household and not valid to current Silhouette Romance™ subscribers. All orders subject to approval.

PRINTED IN U.S.A.

just grazing her skin. ''You look as if you were meant for a ranch.''

Her pulse did a little riff. ''Bowser convinced me that silk and linen would not hold up to mucking out stalls.'' These little detours in conversation were most disconcerting.

''Smart dog.'' His voice slid over her senses as silkily as the shimmering moonlight.

She cleared her throat and started to walk toward her car. ''We need to see if we can overcome Rebecca's fear of dogs.''

''Any other fears we need to deal with?''

''I don't know. I don't know the Hadaway children as well as I'd like to. We'll have to play it by ear.''

''I wasn't talking about the Hadaways.''

Having reached her car, she turned to face him. ''Mr. Whittaker, I sense a change in our relationship. Perhaps, we ought to clear the air.''

His mouth crooked in a half smile. ''I told you when we first met that I appreciate honesty.''

''Then what's going on here? Tonight. Between the two of us. Honestly.''

''Honestly?'' He reached out and brushed an errant wisp of hair from her forehead. ''Miss Little, I'd have to say I'm attracted to you.''

The tingle started at the tips of her ears and ran clear to her toes. She couldn't seem to find her tongue to speak.

''And if further honesty was required,'' he said, running his fingers down the curve of her neck, ''I'd have to admit I feel an urge to kiss you.''

''That would be most unprofessional,'' she whispered, waiting expectantly just the same.

''We're both adults.'' He ran his fingers down her arms, then laced them with her own. ''I think we're capable of keeping the professional separate from the personal.'' He leaned forward and grazed his lips across her forehead.

She could have sworn she saw stars at his touch.

He kissed the outer corner of her eye.

Her lids felt heavy. She wanted to want to tell him to stop. But his touch held an unaccountable healing warmth. She didn't want him to stop. She hadn't felt this whole in ages.

He kissed her earlobe.

She inhaled deeply the faint scent of a musky cologne. His smooth cheek against her own told her that he'd shaved. For her. She felt desired. Womanly. Light-headed.

He kissed the corner of her mouth. A tender but sure kiss.

"Hank…we should think of the kids. Of Friday." Her protest was nothing more than a whisper on the evening breeze.

With the tiniest movement of his lips on hers, he shushed her. "I'm thinking of us. Of now." His warm breath tickled her skin.

She parted her lips, and he covered her mouth with his own.

He was so wrong for her.

Then why did he feel so right?

Releasing her hands, he slipped his arms around her waist. Drew her close into his embrace. Made her feel protected. His small moan at the touch of their tongues told her that he yearned for her the way she did for him.

She slipped her arms around his neck and gave herself up to the moment.

With his deep and searching kiss, it all became clear to her how she'd denied herself this past year. How she'd put her wants and needs on hold. How she'd ignored her hunger.

Hank fed her hunger with the press of his mouth, with the insistent hardness of his body.

When he broke the kiss, he cupped her head in one hand. Pulled her up against his chest so that she rested in the crook of his caress, her face nuzzling against the sinewy warmth of his neck, her blood thrumming hotly in her veins.

"Neesa," he breathed into the moonlight, cradling her gently. "You are one special lady."

He made her feel it. On a personal level she hadn't felt special in far too long a time.

An incredible yearning for him, a yearning for days unwinding in possibility warred within her with a nascent flickering fear. Hank might be looking for a special lady, but she was not the one who could complete his dreams. Not in any permanent way.

And Hank was too special to play with temporarily.

Neesa pulled away. Reluctantly. "I'd better go."

"Stay."

"This is all so sudden."

He stroked her cheek. "Not so sudden when you consider how right it feels." His eyes had gone very dark. Very intense.

She fought the urge to lose herself in them, as well as in his kisses and his embrace, until the day he found out that she could never give him the children—those Whittaker young 'uns—he craved.

Hank deserved a family of his own.

"I need to think," she said, wanting instead to give herself up to mindless kisses.

"Sometimes we think ourselves smack into a dead end."

"Then I need to breathe."

"That I can understand." Smiling gently, he reached out for her hand. "Promise me one thing."

"What?"

"Because of tonight, you won't send someone else in your place Friday."

"I promise." Despite the clear-cut dangers, wild dogs couldn't keep her away. Was she emotionally suicidal?

No, just hungry.

He raised her hand to his lips. Turned it upward. Kissed her palm. "Good."

Her skin tingled icy-hot.

Neesa didn't remember one second of getting into her
car, of driving back to Holly Mount. It seemed that one
moment she was staring up into the desire-filled eyes of a
tall moonlight-etched cowboy and the next moment she was
banging on the front door of her best friend, Claire English.

Claire scowled out the sidelight before opening the door.
When she saw Neesa, her scowl turned to a look of concern. She swung the big door open. "Are you all right?"

"Yes. No. Why would you ask?"

Claire put her hand on Neesa's forehead. "You're
flushed."

"I'm upset."

"Upset? Over what? Is it work?"

Of course Claire would think it was work. Neesa's personal life had been nonexistent ever since the divorce.

"No. It's Hank Whittaker."

"Did he back out of the pilot program?"

"No." Neesa pressed her hands to her cheeks. "He
kissed me."

"Hot dog!"

Neesa grabbed Claire's wrist and shook it hard. "You
don't seem to understand the implications."

"Such as, you might actually begin to cultivate a social
life?" Claire pulled a face. "Poor baby!"

"I came for sympathy, Claire. Cut me some slack."

"Give me something to sympathize with. Telling me a
big hunk of a handsome man kissed you just won't do it,
kiddo."

Neesa paced the English foyer. "He's wrong. He's absolutely wrong for me."

"Why? From the look I got of him at the bus stop, I'd
say there was nothing wrong with that man."

"He wants a family. A big family."

"So?"

"He wants children *of his own*. Just like Paul."

"Honey, he's nothing like Paul." Claire held out her

hand to stay Neesa's pacing. "Paul wouldn't have given your Kids & Animals program the time of day."

That was true.

"Have you actually talked to Hank Whittaker about the kind of family he wants?" Claire's eyes did fill with sympathy now. "Or are you just assuming that a gorgeous macho guy would want to pass down his own set of genes?"

"I've talked to him. He's surprisingly open about wanting to settle down and start a family. And he's not so much macho as...loyal."

"Loyal? I don't understand."

"Blood ties mean the world to him. He's made that clear over and over again. Very emphatically."

"Oh." Claire's one-word response only bolstered Neesa's resolve.

"I vowed I'd never get involved with another man who wasn't committed to remaining childless or to adopting. That man is *not* Hank Whittaker." She rubbed her aching head. "Do you know what is so awful?"

"What, sweetie?"

"He's terrific with kids. With just the right amount of honesty and tact. And a caring that shines through. You can't fake real caring." Her shoulder's slumped. "Oh, Claire, he'll make a wonderful father. And I've never met a better kisser. And tonight he seemed interested... intent...on pursuing a closer relationship with me."

"Then tell him the place you're coming from."

"Tell him about my infertility? I just met him last Friday. Are you crazy?"

"Maybe not so very much. In a short time he seems to have told you some pretty personal stuff."

"I'm afraid."

"Afraid of what?"

"You don't know how cold Paul turned when we learned that...everything...was *my fault*. He turned so cold so fast it was creepy."

"Paul was a jerk." Claire's expression became hard.

"Anyone who would divorce his wife because she couldn't provide the eggs for his children is a jerk."

"I'm not sure I want to risk rejection again," Neesa replied very, very softly.

Claire rubbed Neesa's back in small circles. "You want some ice cream?"

"Real ice cream? Not low-fat or artificially sweetened?"

"Real ice cream. With a gazillion calories."

Neesa sniffed. Tears stung her eyes. She hadn't realized until right now—until it was wholly apparent that she couldn't have him—how much she wanted Hank Whittaker. "Any whipped cream?"

"I'll see what we can find in the fridge." Slipping her arm around her best friend, Claire steered Neesa toward the kitchen.

"Nuts?" she asked hopefully.

"Nuts will be a stretch."

No. Nuts wasn't any kind of stretch. Hank Whittaker, the big strong cowboy with the soft spot in his heart for animals and kids, was making her absolutely nuts.

Hank paced the wide, pine plank flooring of his ranch office. He had work to do: a slew of logging horse paperwork was piled on his desk; demonstration schedules needed to be set up, financial ledgers to balance, industry journals to read. But he could settle down to none of these.

Thoughts of Neesa Little replayed over and over in his mind.

Yes, indeed, but she had wholly captured his attention in only a few short days.

The strangest thing of all seemed to be that she was not the kind of woman he'd thought he and Whispering Pines needed. No, she possessed a delicate sophistication that didn't suit ranch life at all. But how silly that objection seemed in light of her strength of character, her can-do attitude, her devotion to children....

And those kisses.

Her kisses made him wild. Set him on fire. There was no doubt about it.

He needed to talk to her. To hear her voice once more before he settled in for the night. He needed to sense whether their kisses had rattled her world as they had his.

But now he stood frozen like a schoolboy before the phone, not wanting to spook her with his intentions. Stood frozen until he thought of the papers he was supposed to have signed tonight and didn't—as good an excuse as any.

He picked up the receiver, then dialed.

Two rings and a sleepy, "Hello?"

"Did I wake you? This is Hank."

"Yes. A little."

"Sorry." He wasn't, particularly. He smiled to himself to picture her half-awake and muzzy with dreams. "I just wondered about the papers I was supposed to sign tonight. Were they important enough for me to meet you at your office tomorrow?"

"No!" Her response was immediate. She seemed wide awake now. "No, Friday will be soon enough."

"Oh." The prospect of waiting a whole day and night to see her again was not to his liking. "Neesa, about tonight—"

"I'm sorry—"

"You are?"

"Well, yes and no."

"Tell me about the no part." He was a sucker for optimism.

"I'd be a fool not to admit the chemistry."

"But you're sorry because…"

"Because we're working together in a professional setting."

"So you're telling me I need to either dump the Hadaways or my feelings for you?"

"Hank, I'm not issuing ultimatums."

"I want the Hadaways and me to work *and* I want you and me to work."

She laughed, and the lilting sound over the phone line was music to his ears. "Are you always this forthright?"

"When the stakes are high enough."

"What exactly do you see as the stakes...where I'm concerned?"

"All I'm asking is to be able to follow this...this chemistry, as you call it, as far as it takes us."

She let out a long, low breath.

"If it eases your mind any, all this has taken me by surprise, too," he offered.

"Quite frankly, Mr. Whittaker, you take my breath away."

"That's my intention, Miss Little." Even as the words slipped from his lips, Hank couldn't believe he'd uttered them.

Chapter Seven

If Neesa had been worried about Hank acting all gooey-eyed when she saw him next, she needn't have. Despite his kisses and his unexpected phone call Wednesday night, Friday morning showed no personality change. He was still a long, tall cowboy with an inscrutable gaze and a habit of speaking only when he had something to say. He'd greeted the Hadaway children and her with the same reserved welcome he'd exhibited on Tuesday. And except for signing the necessary agency papers, he hadn't tried to get her alone. Hadn't acted in any way except absolutely professional.

She had to admit to surprise, admiration, relief…and a tiny, tiny sliver of disappointment.

An added surprise was that for this morning he'd put Whispering Pines' entire crew—himself, Reba, Willy and Tucker—at her disposal, guaranteeing a one-on-one child, adult ratio. He seemed to have a natural-born teacher's, or a prospective father's, instinct when it came to children and a generosity of spirit to match. When he'd gathered them all at the big kitchen table to discuss the work detail, he'd included the children in the decision-making, had treated them as valued ranch hands. Of course, as they planned, Reba had stuffed them with fresh fruit, sticky buns and milk. Neesa had never before envisioned ranch hands with milk and icing mustaches, but the process had seemed to work for the most part. For today, Martin was to work with Willy cleaning out stalls. Nell was to work with Reba in the kitchen garden. Thomas was to work with Tucker tending to the mule's lame leg. Carlie was to help Hank shear the three sheep. And Rebecca was to work with Neesa feeding the cat and kittens, then gathering hens' eggs.

Everything went smoothly just until they all moved to disperse.

It was then that Hank reached across the table, chucked Rebecca under the chin and said softly, "You all right, sugah?"

"Why wouldn't she be?" Martin's protective instincts immediately went into overdrive.

"Oh, just a couple dark circles highlighting those big, beautiful eyes." Hank winked at Rebecca, and she dimpled.

Martin scowled. "She wakes up with nightmares."

Hank didn't rise to the boy's confrontational tone. Instead he said to the four-year-old, "Now don't let Miss Neesa work you too hard today, you hear?"

Rebecca silently bobbed her head up and down in agreement.

"I don't know how taking care of a bunch of reject animals is going to help her any," Martin muttered. This was the second time in as many days that he'd said as much. Clearly, it was some kind of challenge to Hank.

When Hank let the challenge die, Neesa mentally blessed him for his patience.

Willy diverted Martin's attention with a question, defusing the boy's hostility. The pairing of the tall, lanky teenager with the tiny old man had been a stroke of genius. Nobody could remain angry at the ancient foreman with the crusty sense of humor. And the head of the Hadaways certainly wouldn't feel intimidated by him sizewise. Martin shot Hank one last menacing look before leaving with Willy.

"Well, Carlie," Hank asked, "are you ready to shear some sheep?"

His words were for the girl, but his parting glance, full of a gentle intensity, was for Neesa. It seemed to say that things would work out.

As Neesa held out her hand to Rebecca, she felt an unmistakable longing rise within her. A longing to share her hopes and fears with a man like Hank Whittaker. Despite all reason, she found herself increasingly attracted to him.

The second emotional jolt came when Rebecca slipped her tiny hand into Neesa's. The warmth of the child's touch and the trust in her eyes pushed every biological button Neesa had so carefully guarded with child safety locks.

"Miss Neesa, we're not gonna feed that big ol' dog, are we?"

"No, 'Becca. Not until you tell me or Hank you want to."

"I like Hank."

"So do I, sweetie." Neesa held the kitchen screen door open for the child. "So do I."

As they walked hand in hand across the barnyard, Neesa could hear activity buzzing about them and could feel a strange contentment, commensurate with the sound, rise within her. For a year she'd felt anything but content. Driven in work, yes. Lonely in her personal life, yes. But content? Not for one minute. Until now. She hoped Whispering Pines would work as a healing balm for the children as it seemed to work for her.

But was it really the ranch working the magic...or the rancher?

Neesa pushed that pesky thought to the back of her mind as she and Rebecca headed to the barn to feed the ginger mama and her kittens. Thankfully, Hank would be busy with Carlie and sheepshearing and wouldn't prove an un-settling presence this morning.

Stepping through the barn's big doorway, however, Neesa ran smack up against the cowboy's hard frame.

"Now, Carlie," he said with a twinkle in his eye as he reached out to steady Neesa, "that's just what I was telling you about interesting things always popping up on a ranch." He tipped his Stetson back on his head. "What can I do for you, Miss Neesa?"

His unwavering gaze never failed to give her heart a run for its money. "We were looking for the cat chow. You said it was in the barn."

"Right here." He turned to reveal a cupboard from which it appeared he'd just retrieved the sheep shears. The cat chow box stood on the middle shelf.

Neesa reached for it, noting that Hank didn't give her much room to maneuver. In fact, to do so, she needed to brush up against his broad chest. Avoiding eye contact and quickly suppressing the pleasurable surge that took place deep within her, she grasped the chow box, then handed it to Rebecca.

"How will we find the kitties?" Rebecca asked.

"Just rattle that box," Hank replied, with a grin, "and they'll find you."

"I want to stay and watch." Animation banished the haunted look Carlie's face usually showed.

"And I want to see Carlie's sheep," Rebecca insisted.

"Then there's only one thing to do." Hank caught Neesa's gaze and held it. "Team up. The four of us."

"Yeah!" the girls agreed unison.

Yeah, thought Neesa. Just what I need—a morning spent in Father Goose's company.

"Miss Neesa?" Hank fairly beamed down at her.

"Of course, if that's what the girls want." It wasn't—and *was* unfortunately—exactly what she wanted.

Rebecca shook the cat chow box. The resulting rattle

brought the ginger mama and her kittens at a run. Both girls giggled.

Hank spread a newspaper from a stack in the cupboard on the floor. "Sprinkle it around on the paper so they all get some. When they've finished eating, you can pet them." He glanced at Neesa. "There's nothing like a little TLC to start the day."

She felt prickly heat rise from the neckband of her T-shirt.

Hank watched the girls engrossed in their simple task and took pleasure in their childish joy. He watched Neesa flush a pretty pink and took immense pleasure in her discomfort. It wasn't that he was a man who normally enjoyed the unease of any living body, animal or human. But in this instance, Neesa coloring told him that she wasn't indifferent to his attentions.

His attentions would have to be subtle today, for he had no intention of stepping outside the professional with Miss Neesa Little in front of the children. Neither had he any intention of jeopardizing Kids & Animals. It wasn't only that he'd lose Neesa's company. Actually, he could woo her more easily if they weren't working together. No, his resolve ran deeper: he didn't want to risk losing the Hadaways. In a short time, they had added considerably—and surprisingly—to the happy expectation and sense of challenge he experienced in getting out of bed each morning.

He had plain looked forward to today.

Which didn't mean he wouldn't try to find himself in Neesa's company whenever the opportunity arose.

Willy and Martin marched by, shovels slung over their shoulders. "Best damned job on the ranch, if you ask me," the flinty foreman was saying. "Mucking out stalls, you can drain every cussed ill thought out of your body before midday meal."

Martin didn't look convinced, but there was no sign of the macho posturing look he always threw Hank. And Willy was right. Physical labor did act as a great stress reliever. Hank only hoped the old man would curb his off-color jokes.

"I just love these kitties!" Rebecca sat on the packed dirt of the barn floor as three of the kittens played on her lap. It seemed those three would rather get loved than fed.

Smart kittens.

Turning to Neesa, Hank caught a look of absolute longing in her eyes as she watched the little girl. If he didn't miss his guess, she wanted what he wanted: a family of her own.

"I like the mama," Carlie said ever so softly, her voice catching. "Mamas are special."

Neesa blinked hard as if suppressing tears. Even so, the soft blue of her eyes turned dark. Cloudy. Pained. Hank wondered if she'd responded simply to the Hadaways' plight, or to some hidden hurt in her past. He vowed to find out.

"This mama's extra special," Hank said, bending to stroke the ginger cat. "Not only does she keep her kittens fed and clean, but she keeps the barn free from mice."

"A career woman!" Neesa seemed to have regained her composure with an added measure of sass.

"Exactly!" Lordy, but he liked basking in her sunny company. "Girls, are you ready to go check on the chicken factory?"

"The chicken factory?" Carlie wrinkled her nose.

"Yup. Where they make the eggs that Reba puts into those sticky buns."

"Will I see the kitties again?" Rebecca seemed to hesitate.

"Darlin', knowing there's a playmate like you around, they won't stray far." The insecurities and doubts that flickered on and off the Hadaway faces purely tore at his heart.

"Are there any baby chickens?"

"Not yet."

"What do you mean?" Rebecca's four-year-old attention span seemed to have shifted.

"You have to come to the henhouse to see."

Eagerly Rebecca slipped her hand into Neesa's, and Hank was struck by a similarity in coloring between the woman and child as well as a corresponding delicacy of build. If he didn't know better, he might almost mistake them for mother and daughter.

He suppressed a thought as to what a daughter born to Neesa and him might look like.

Taking the lead around the barn to the henhouse, he smiled as Carlie fairly danced about him. Her enthusiasm hung rich with associations in the air. When he was seven, his whole universe revolved around family, animals, the land and plenty of fresh air. For the last few years, he'd had the last three in spades. It was time to settle down and concentrate on the first.

It didn't hurt his plans to feast his eyes on Miss Neesa Little. Oh, no, it didn't. Not one bit.

He had to duck to enter the henhouse. Usually, Reba collected the eggs. "This is kind of like an Easter egg hunt," he said to the girls. "Only the eggs aren't chocolate, they're sometimes warm, and they can break easily." Reaching into a nesting box, he closed his fingers around an example, then held it aloft.

He was rewarded by a brilliant smile from Neesa. "I use those egg substitutes from the freezer. Not half as much fun to gather."

Chuckling, he lifted Rebecca who immediately spotted an egg.

"Why is that hen all by herself in that closed-in box?" Carlie wanted to know.

"Because she's broody."

"Sometimes Martin says I'm moody."

"Not moody, sweetheart. Broody. She's sitting on a nest of eggs that will turn into chicks."

"I want to see!" Rebecca twisted in his arms.

"Only when the eggs hatch. Right now we have to let her be. Let her settle in to prepare for raising a family."

He wondered if Neesa could see beneath the surface to the analogy. Willy, Reba and even his brother Brett had long observed what had only recently become obvious to himself: he, too, was nesting.

Amazing.

One of the free-range Whittaker boys had grown tired of bachelorhood.

Carlie's expression suddenly showed troubled thoughts. "Miss Neesa, will we still be here when the chicks are born?"

"Absolutely." With a reassuring glance at Carlie, Neesa reached for one of the egg baskets hanging in the rafters.

It struck Hank that he could do something about the impermanence of relationships in his life—going from bachelorhood to married life if he so chose. The Hadaway children obviously viewed impermanence as inevitable, because their fates were held in the hands of others. That realization gave Hank pause, and, even though the five weren't blood kin, his protective instincts kicked in.

Neesa had begun to help the girls collect the eggs from his dozen or so layers. The sight struck him as pleasantly odd. It wasn't often he found himself surrounded by femininity. Or noticed it much. Heck, Willy, Tucker…and he even treated Reba as one of the boys. He'd been blind, for sure. Perhaps it had taken the quiet Miss Little to make him see.

"How many sticky buns will this make?" With an immensely satisfied look on her face, Carlie held the full egg basket forward.

"Enough to give you one terrific bellyache." Hank was glad to see the girl's enthusiasm restored.

Neesa grinned. "Do you think Miss Reba might teach the girls and me next time she makes the sticky buns?"

"Let's bring these to her and ask."

"Does the Easter bunny collect eggs this way?" Rebecca screwed up her face at the prospect.

"Help me, Miss Neesa," Hank said with a laugh. "We've wandered beyond my range of expertise."

Quite frankly, in her presence his thoughts had wandered also—beyond egg gathering to the play of shadow and light on Neesa's blond hair, on her china-doll features, on her soft, rosy lips. It wasn't but two days ago that he'd kissed those lips....

"Hank?" Rebecca tugged at his jeans.

It was downright embarrassing to be caught daydreaming—about sweet, slow kisses, no less—in a henhouse.

Neesa stared at Hank in fascination as he tried to collect his thoughts. It almost seemed as if he was as distracted by her as she was by him.

Now that was a dangerous prospect.

"I think Easter bunnies are chock-full of secrets," she offered in response to his silence. "And how they get their eggs is just one of them. Let's get these eggs to Miss Reba and ask her if she'll teach us to make sticky buns on Tuesday."

"Thomas'll want to know how, too." Rebecca turned her attention to Neesa.

"Martin won't," Carlie added quickly.

"You never know." Neesa held out the egg basket so that Rebecca could share the handle with her. "If Miss Reba agrees, we'll make it an open boy-girl class."

"Hank, too?"

Hank almost looked eager.

"No," Neesa replied. "I think by next Tuesday we'll know our way around the ranch enough so that Hank, Willy and Tucker can get back to their work."

"Oh, I don't know," Hank countered with a lazy grin. "Miss Reba's sticky buns have been a mystery to me for far too long."

"Kinda like the Easter bunny and his eggs." Rebecca took hold of the egg basket in one hand and Hank's hand with the other. Of all the children, she was the most ready to settle into life on Whispering Pines.

Neesa rued Hank's revelation that he had no need to consider adoption.

She'd certainly considered adopting the Hadaways. But she knew her single-parent status would prove inadequate to an instant family of five. Still, that didn't stop her from the pain of dreaming.

Neesa knew that her friend Claire wondered why she didn't save herself from any such pain by pursuing another career—a career away from children. But Claire had kind and loving Robert. She'd never felt less a woman because her husband couldn't stomach her infertility. She'd never been abandoned because she'd been found biologically lacking. But Neesa had been. And having been abandoned in marriage, she'd vowed not to abandon already abandoned children. She might move out of the kid-filled Holly Mount subdivision, but she wasn't going to move out on the Hadaways.

The two adults and two girls walked past the paddock where Tucker was instructing Thomas on the fine points of getting to know Gizmo, the mule. Thomas seemed enthralled. Then, as they approached the back door to the ranch by way of the kitchen garden, Neesa heard the most enchanting sound: two voices raised in song, one woman's, one girl's, singing simple old-time folk tunes. When Nell saw the new arrivals, however, she quickly stopped singing and lowered her gaze to the garden plants at her feet.

"That was beautiful!" Neesa exclaimed. "I didn't know you sang so well, Nell."

"She has a lovely voice." Reba wiped her hands on her apron. "It's a pleasure to work with her."

Nell, never looking up, blushed, but smiled nonetheless.

Oh, there was hope for this program yet, Neesa thought happily.

"We brought you eggs!" Rebecca couldn't contain herself.

"And we want lessons making sticky buns!" Carlie couldn't, either.

"And I want to lick the spoon!" Hank winked at Neesa.

My, my, but that man had a way of nuzzling right into a woman's heart.

"Anytime," Reba replied, a grandmotherly smile wreathing her features.

"Now?" All three girls spoke at once.

"What about the garden?"

Nell seemed to change her mind. "I do love the garden...."

"And the sheep?" Hank asked.

"Too many choices." Carlie looked crestfallen.

Hank bent to ruffle her hair. "Then you'll just have to come back again and again until you've tried everything."

Bless his heart.

All three girls exchanged hopeful glances.

Hank held the shears aloft. "Sheepshearing?"

"Sheepshearing!"

Neesa wondered when the last time was that the Hadaways had been given so many options, so many new experiences, so much attention.

Thinking of her own solitary life, she could identify with them and a sense of newfound riches.

The sheepshearing had been a success as had the other chores. The Hadaways were obviously tired and hot and hungry but supremely satisfied—even Martin—as children and adults, minus Reba, gathered at the outdoor spigot and horse trough to wash up for the midday meal.   •

Neesa couldn't have recounted the steps in shearing if her life had depended upon it. All morning she'd been mesmerized on the one hand by Carlie and Rebecca's total absorption in new and fascinating tasks and on the other hand by Hank's beautiful way with children, his absolute ease in the out-of-doors and a certain sexy just-you-wait attitude that underlined every word he spoke directly to her, every glance he passed her way.

If the idea wasn't so wholly preposterous, she might actually think she was falling in love with him.

"I was thinking of hanging a tire swing in the barn doorway," Hank said, turning on the tap. "You kids could help me rig it."

The Hadaways didn't say anything, as if unwilling to hope, but they smiled, eyes averted, and nudged each other. All except Martin. He remained aloof.

"Won't it block the barn door?" Neesa asked.

"Nah." Hank splashed water on his face. "We always had one there when my brothers and I were kids. The adults knew when to pin it back, and we learned when we could swing and when to get out of the big folks' way." He grinned at her, his hair all spiky and wet, his tanned skin glistening in the noonday sun, his teeth a confident slash of white. "Besides, the adults sitting in rockers on the veranda can keep an eye on the kids."

It was just like him to be this wise—letting the kids have a little freedom while never forgetting that the adults were in charge. He *would* make a good father one day. Too bad he would be someone else's husband.

"Okay, let me count noses," he ordered as the kids slurped and slopped and horsed around like…like kids!…in the water. "Heads up!"

The Hadaways looked up expectantly.

"Where's Rebecca?" Neesa asked. "She was at my side just a second ago."

Everyone looked around, but Rebecca was nowhere to be seen.

"Maybe she scooted in to see Reba and check on dinner," Willy suggested. "I'll go check."

"No sticking your fingers in the banana pudding while you're checking," Hank warned with a wink to the kids as he passed out clean towels Reba had left near the spigot.

His nonchalant air didn't fool Neesa one bit. His gaze held a flicker of worry as he cast a quick glance around the barnyard. He wasn't the only one on alert. Martin had gone tense and was doing his own visual check of the surrounding area.

It wasn't long before Willy stuck his head out the front doorway. "Reba's checking to see if she's picking flowers in the kitchen garden. I'll run out to the pasture to see if she's with the sheep."

"*Rebecca!*" Martin shouted, looking around wildly, his hands clenched at his side.

Hank reached out to lay a hand on the boy's shoulder. "She's not gone far. She was right here a minute ago."

His face a mask of fury, Martin twisted away from Hank's touch. "This is all your damn fault!"

"Watch your language, son." Hank spoke slowly, patiently but with unmistakable authority.

"I'm not your son," Martin growled, his eyes two angry slits, his features contemptuous.

"It appears not. But you'll curb your tongue nonetheless." Hank turned to Carlie. "Sweetheart, will you go check the henhouse to see if Rebecca's looking for more eggs?"

"Sure." The girl started across the yard, but Martin stopped her with an outstretched hand. "Stay here, Carlie." Spitting out his words, the teenager focused on Hank in an obvious power play. "You're not sending her to get lost, too."

"We haven't lost Rebecca," Neesa insisted. Martin was blowing the whole situation out of proportion and, Neesa feared, blowing Kids & Animals into treacherous waters. He might just destroy his own chances for a little happiness. "There are enough of us to find her before she wanders too far."

"I'll go with Carlie to look in the henhouse, Miss Neesa," Nell offered.

"She's not the boss of the Hadaways, Nell. I am." Martin seemed to get angrier by the minute. "And don't forget she's the one who forced us into this stupid situation in the first place."

Tucker took Thomas's hand. "We'll take a walk down the lane to see if she might have gone exploring."

"Don't you go with him, Thomas!" Martin shrieked.

"Martin. Enough." Neesa stepped toward the teenager, but refrained from touching him in his present agitated state. Clearly his world as he knew it was shifting. Clearly the shift unnerved him. "The more time we spend arguing, the less time we spend looking for—"

"*Shut up!*"

"No. *You* be still." Hank was at Neesa's side in a second, towering over both Martin and herself. Yet even he didn't risk touching the boy. He seemed to hold his words in check deliberately. "Get a grip, Martin. You aren't the center of attention here. Rebecca is. We're all going to set out to find her now. You can help or you can feel sorry for yourself. Either way, you'll apologize to Miss Neesa before you sit down to eat."

"It's okay, Hank," Neesa's concern was first for Rebecca's physical welfare, then for Martin's emotional state.

"No, it isn't, Neesa." Hank stared pointedly at Martin. "Being parentless is no excuse for being thoughtless."

Wheeling about, Martin ran off toward the barn.

Freed from the power struggle, Nell and Carlie hustled hand in hand toward the henhouse as Tucker and Thomas trotted down the lane.

The calls of "Rebecca!" rang in Neesa's ears. Worry pulsed in her veins. She turned to Hank. "Now we've lost a second child."

"We haven't lost anyone."

"You overstepped your bounds just now. With Martin." She was nothing if not an advocate for the children.

"I don't see it that way. The boy lost control. He needed to see that and stand accountable for his actions."

"I wasn't insulted."

"You should have been. Aren't you the one trying to teach them a two-way respect? Responsibility?"

"I'm trying to enrich their lives." She turned to leave. "I need to help find Rebecca."

Hank grasped her wrist to stop her. "There are seven people looking for Rebecca. They'll find her. We need to set some ground rules."

"Obviously." Tension mounting in every limb, she looked him directly in the eyes. "You're the sponsor here. You provide the animals and the site. I provide the individual supervision."

"I'm not allowed to guide them, to act as role model?"

"You're not their father."

"You're not their mother."

"Martin was obviously worried. He needed reassurance, not a lecture on manners."

"He needs to learn to cope with his emotions." Hank reached out with his free hand and gently brushed her cheek with his fingertips. "It was a teenage outburst, Neesa. I treated him no better and no worse than I would have treated my own son. What are you so afraid of?"

"That because he's not your own son, he'll feel raw rejection." As she had with Paul. "The Hadaways have felt far too much rejection already." As she had in her marriage. Somehow Hank's acceptance of the five children had become jumbled crazily in her mind with his acceptance of her. As is. Flaws and all.

"You'll find I'm a fair man." He released her wrist, but slid his fingers down to entwine with hers. "Give me a break. Let me get involved."

"So you can break their hearts when it comes time for them to leave?"

"There's a time for everything." He slipped his hand from hers. "I can't make unreasonable promises, Neesa."

"Then don't set yourself up as a father figure. The animals will have to be enough."

The muscles in his jaw twitched at the same moment the midnight blue of his eyes went flat and unreadable. "I'm going to check the barn. Rebecca may have gone back to see the kittens one last time.''

He turned, then strode across the barnyard, the set of his shoulders stiff.

Neesa hastened to follow him. Had Martin—and then she—torpedoed Kids & Animals? She would never forgive herself if she turned out to be the cause of this wonderful opportunity being snatched from the Hadaways. But how could she let Hank get more involved than the normal sponsor? He'd admitted that he was ready to settle down and raise a family. Children *of his own*. Then where would the Hadaways be? Looking for a new, temporary situation. Again.

As emotionally tricky as it was to expose her own heart to Hank Whittaker, it was five times more dangerous to expose the hearts of Martin, Nell, Thomas, Carlie and Rebecca.

Ahead, she saw Hank pause in the barn doorway. Turning to her, he waved her forward with one hand as he held a finger of the other to his lips. Curiosity got the better of her worries. She hurried to his side.

It took a moment for her eyes to adjust to the shadows within the barn. But when they did, she saw Martin leaning against the side of the first stall, staring intently within.

Neesa followed his gaze and spied, on the freshly spread hay, Rebecca asleep, the ginger mama cat and her kittens curled protectively about her. The child's face held a look of utter trust and relaxation. The circles under her eyes seemed less intense somehow.

A softness had come over Martin's features. ''She never sleeps this soundly at the home,'' he said, his words a gravelly whisper.

''Maybe the animals can do some good, after all.'' Hank didn't move to enter either child's space.

Martin would admit to nothing, but by the way he hastily swiped at the corner of one eye, Neesa could tell he had been moved.

"I'll stay with her while you eat," she offered. "Unless you think she'd rather have you."

"No...she trusts you." The boy glanced at Hank then back at Neesa. "I'm sorry if I made you think otherwise."

It was an apology.

Neesa looked at Hank to see if he was going to press the issue further.

He didn't look at her. "I'll tell the others she's okay," he said, turning to leave.

"I was worried." Martin paused as he passed her a couple of moments later.

"I know."

"Do you have brothers and sisters?"

"No." Perhaps that was why she longed so for a family.

"Then you might not understand. Blood is thicker than water. Thicker than anything."

It might be thick, but it certainly wasn't simple.

Chapter Eight

Friday night Hank found an agency folder that Neesa had left behind at his ranch. Unlike Wednesday, when he'd hesitated to call her, he got into his truck and drove straight to Holly Mount subdivision, compelled more by the fact that he wouldn't see her until Tuesday than by the possibility that she might miss the paperwork. In his opinion, she and he had to iron out some issues that had been left unresolved that afternoon.

One issue had to do with his wanting her.

Oh, he wanted Neesa Little, yes.

But his wanting had turned complicated.

He couldn't deny the simple physical attraction he felt for her. The crackle in the air when she was around. The ache when she wasn't. He'd discovered thoughts of her delicate beauty creeping into his dreams, troubling his sleep, leaving his mornings stiff and unfulfilled.

Neither could he deny the pure emotional attraction he felt for her. He admired her and her work. He liked talking to her. He trusted her. He'd more than once caught himself in the middle of ranch operations or business forecasting, wanting to talk out a new wrinkle with her. As if she were a given part of his future. Heck, she'd even gotten him talking about some pretty personal stuff. Settling down. Raising a family. It had felt surprisingly natural to open up with her.

But there were things in their budding relationship that gave him pause. The fact that he had known her only one week today was near the top of the list. That she was at the same time so easy to know and so difficult to know was next in line.

For instance, take her dealings with the Hadaways. Mixed signals.

Neesa wanted his help with the five children...but she didn't. She seemed almost as if she wanted to expose them to Hank's structured life, and at the same time she tried to protect them from any simple disciplinary action he might take. She wanted him to act as a role model, but she discouraged him from acting too much like a father. She wanted the children to get the most out of their Whispering Pines experience, yet she helped them build a protective wall around their feelings. He didn't understand these mixed signals.

Perhaps he'd made her wary when he'd talked openly about his nesting urges. She did seem skittish on that front. But he didn't see where his participation in Kids & Animals and his wanting a family of his own were mutually exclusive.

The biggest concern dogging Hank's thoughts, however, had less to do with what Neesa said or did than with what she didn't do, didn't say. While he'd spoken about his innermost feelings, she'd listened. On the other hand, she'd told him very little about her own personal hopes and dreams. And even less about her past. An occasional, swift look of pain in her blue eyes was the only hint he had that her life hadn't been all upscale and easygoing. Too, he'd sensed a deep emotional reticence about her anytime things began to heat up physically between them.

He was a proud man, who didn't want to play the fool rushing in where his attentions weren't wanted. Before he found himself head over heels, he definitely needed to clear the air with Neesa Little.

He pulled into her driveway and grabbed the agency folder.

Walking up to the front door, he found himself, despite frequent mental admonitions to play it cool, eager to see her. He rang the bell and felt the first wave of self-consciousness wash over him.

When she opened the door, barefoot, in cutoff short shorts that highlighted her shapely legs and a big T-shirt that purely swallowed her up, her features vulnerable, her blond hair tousled and her free hand holding a shiny red lollipop, he fought for breath.

"I didn't know you liked red lollipops." It was a dumb thing to say. He knew it the minute it slipped out of his mouth. But, as the moths hovering about her front light were his witness, it was the only thing with any sense that came to mind. He was that tongue-tied.

She hesitated. "Care to join me?"

"Sure." Even though he disliked red lollipops.

Glancing at the folder he held in his hand, she opened the door wider.

"You forgot this at the ranch today." He wanted to take her in his arms.

"I was just about to go over my notes."

"Maybe we could talk about the day. What went right. What went wrong." He wanted to kiss away the tiny furrow that creased her brow.

"Martin." She sighed.

"One of many topics." He wanted to tell her that sometimes he thought they weren't just talking about the Hadaways.

She turned, then led him into a massive cathedral-ceilinged family room decorated all in white. It was expensive looking. And sterile.

At six foot three, he felt dwarfed. "I don't mean to be rude, but somehow I don't picture this as you."

"It isn't." She walked to built-in shelving that housed a wet bar. "It was designed for corporate entertaining." She tilted her head enigmatically. "This was my last red lollipop. Can I offer you a soft drink instead?"

"Sure. Anything you have that's cold." He wanted to find the key to unlock her reserve. Wanted her to feel as easy with him as he did with her. But he felt stymied. Why did things between men and women have to be so complicated? Why did you always have to endure this predance ritual before you could get down to the honest holding?

She handed him a cola. "Are you angry with me?"

"Me? Angry with you?"

"It seemed as if, earlier today, we kind of locked horns in a power struggle."

"How can there be a power struggle when we both want what's best for the Hadaways?"

"Do we?" Like a small, colorful bird dwarfed by her surroundings, she perched on the edge of the big white sofa.

"I think so. We just have different parenting styles."

"The Hadaways are not our children."

"Don't take this the wrong way." He took a seat in a chair separated from her by a huge glass coffee table covered with folders, papers and her laptop. The mess was the only thing that made the room look even faintly homey. "But how we behave around the Hadaways gives a sneak preview of how we'll behave as parents."

She stiffened. "They aren't guinea pigs."

"I never meant to suggest that they were."

"And we aren't trying out for parent of the year." Those storm clouds were back in her eyes.

"I didn't mean to suggest that either."

"Then what are you suggesting?"

That they'd again slipped away from talking only about the Hadaways.

Before he could reply, she continued quickly as if perhaps she didn't want to hear his answer. "This is going to be a more complicated process than either you or I anticipated," she said, rubbing her arms with a little shiver. "It's only normal we both bring a certain amount of personal history and emotional baggage to it."

"Yes." For fear of making her uneasy enough to drop the subject, he said no more.

"Care to talk about it?" she asked, her manner straightforward, but her body language on alert.

He did. This might be the key he'd been searching for. He nodded.

She twisted the hem of her T-shirt. "I think you've been fairly honest with me. You've told me you're ready for a wife and family of your own. That lets me know where the Hadaways stand—"

"Now, wait a minute. If you're suggesting one rules out the other, why should it?"

"Your wife might not be as understanding as Reba, Willy and Tucker where Kids & Animals are concerned."

Shaking his head, he flashed her a grin. "You're not giving me much credit in the wife-shopping department." In fact, he wished she'd pay a little more attention to the signals he'd been sending out.

She colored prettily, but held his gaze. "You don't know how long I've struggled to place these children, even temporarily. Even part-time. I want so much for this program to succeed. For them."

"So do I. Why are you counting on failure?"

She looked down at her hands. "Because this whole idea of blood being thicker than water is such a double-edged sword."

He was taken back by the pain in her words.

Neesa took her time looking up. She knew how Hank felt about biological ties. About the same way Martin did. She didn't mean to insult or even to minimize their feelings on the matter. But fate had made her see the other side of the coin. If Hank supposedly wanted honesty, she would be honest: because of personal circumstances that she intended to keep private, she was an advocate for stitching together families in any way possible.

"I'm talking about the pain of rejection. Rejection from any quarter," she said, taking an honest but alternate approach, unwilling to wander too closely to the subject of her infertility. She didn't want this man's pity. Or the possibility of his rejection.

"You sound as if you're talking from experience." His voice reached out to her, deep and rich.

"I am." She looked up. Right into dark eyes so still she could almost see her reflection in them. "My husband left me a year ago."

He didn't bat an eyelash. "My fiancée left me."

Stunned by his openness, she didn't know how to respond to this admission. "I'm not telling you so you'll say, 'Poor Neesa.'"

He grinned. A sexy, soul stirring grin. "Believe me. It never occurred to me to say that."

"The terrains of the heart don't make for easy traveling." Although this man, disconcertingly enough, seemed more willing than most to give the journey a try.

He leaned forward in his chair. "Who are you more afraid for, Neesa? For the Hadaways or for yourself?"

"I'm not afraid." She looked long and hard at him, wondering how she could explain the jumble of her feelings without leaving herself totally vulnerable. "It's just that I understand the precarious position the Hadaways find themselves in. To a lesser degree, I was abandoned. I understand how difficult it is to trust again."

"I'm asking you to trust me." The intensity of his regard washed over her. It was the same look he'd given her that first morning at the bus stop. The one that saw deep within her.

"With the Hadaways," she said.

"Where they're concerned, yes. And also where you're concerned."

"Me?"

"You."

"Professionally, you mean."

"I'd rather mean personally." He rose, then came slowly round the coffee table to sit beside her. "Seems we have two agendas here, Neesa."

The room suddenly felt extremely warm. "I didn't expect this. You. Me. The personal side of it."

"I didn't expect it, either, but you can't tell me it's impossible."

Impossible. That it was.

Sitting next to him, she held herself rigid, all the while wanting to let herself go. For the past year she'd bottled so much emotion tightly within, not even sharing it with Claire. Why did she now feel compelled to open up with this man? Hank Whittaker. Who could never be Mister Right.

She felt the touch of his fingertips on her arm and realized she was trembling.

"What's wrong?" His eyes promised he would understand.

Perhaps he would...to a point.

Still, she made a stab at honesty. "When Paul left me," she replied cautiously, "he left me feeling less than a whole woman. I haven't been part of a relationship since." She hazarded a smile. "I guess I'm rusty."

He gently ran the pad of his thumb over her mouth. "Believe me, the woman I kissed Wednesday was a whole woman. And definitely not rusty."

She swallowed hard.

"In fact, she's the most attractive woman I've ever met," he whispered as he leaned forward and softly kissed the corner of her mouth.

Her eyes closed and crossed. "I...I wasn't fishing."

"I wasn't feeding you a line." He ran his fingers up the back of her neck and into her hair.

More than anything in the world she wanted to touch

him. Wanted to make certain that he was real. That this was no fantasy born of her yearnings. Tentatively she reached out and placed her hand on his chest. Felt his warmth under the fabric of his shirt. Felt the rise and fall of his breathing. The regular beat of his heart. He was so strong and so very, very compelling.

She wanted to lose herself in him.

He lifted her chin so that she had to look directly into his eyes. "Do you know the only thing wrong with Wednesday's kisses?"

She shook her head. Funny, but she couldn't think of a single fault.

Mischief twinkled in the depths of those midnight blues. "They gave me a powerful hunger for more."

Oh, my.

She clutched at sanity. "Hank, the kids!"

"I don't see any kids." He kissed the tip of her nose. "It's just you and me, but if you want me to stop—"

"No!" She didn't. She wanted this moment—selfishly perhaps—all for herself.

He drew her to him. Drew her into the circle of his arms. Then he found her mouth and claimed her.

This kiss was not the sweet and simple kiss of Wednesday. This kiss was filled with electricity and complex passion. Whereas Wednesday's kiss was a question, this kiss was a promise. This kiss brooked no turning back.

Threading her fingers in Hank's hair, Neesa pressed herself to him. He made a sound deep in his throat, a primitive and territorial sound. Her tongue sought his. Despite all the warning bells, he was what she wanted. Her body thrummed in response to his touch.

And his touch had grown bolder.

"You are so soft," he murmured huskily in her ear as he ran his hand possessively up her outer thigh.

And he was so hard. The planes of his face. The muscles of his chest and arms. She felt dizzy with exploring him. Her fingers ached to know this man. "Hank..." She whispered his name in affirmation. Thought only of what she could give him. Repressed what she could not. He was hers for the moment. For right now.

Drawing back just a little, he looked down at her in his arms. A dark lock of hair had fallen over his forehead, making him look the rogue. His eyes held a smoldering duskiness. His lips looked well kissed. "Do you know you've been driving me crazy since the first time I laid eyes on you? At the bus stop."

Running her finger lightly around the outline of his mouth, she shuddered with pleasure when he nipped her. "Is that so?" She felt alive for the first time in years.

He lowered his mouth to hers and said so softly it tickled her lips, "Yes, ma'am."

Unable to withstand the delicious tease, she cupped his head in her hands. Drew him close. Kissed him full and with abandon.

He growled in response, his hand finding its way under her loose T-shirt.

Her bare flesh tingled as he caressed upward. As she felt his callused palm lovingly stroke her stomach, her side, her back, then her breast.

With Hank she felt every inch a woman. Desired. Cherished.

On fire.

Lordy, it was true what they said about bells ringing.

The pounding on her front door, however, broke the spell.

"Neesa!" Claire's voice. "I know you're in there! Open up! Robert has class tonight, and I forgot my key!"

The doorbell rang double-time.

With a long, low groan, Hank released Neesa. "I don't suppose you could just slip her the key through the mail slot?"

"With your truck in the yard? Not a chance." Giggling, Neesa fussed at her rumpled clothing. "Claire has a need *to know.*"

When she stood, he grasped her hand. "Know that I'm crazy about you."

She resisted the urge to fall back into his arms, leaving her best friend huffing and puffing on her doorstep. "Well, I'm crazy to let myself feel this way about you—"

"But you're not going to fight it. This feeling." It was no question.

Honesty. He'd said he wanted honesty. And his dark gaze held on to her as firmly as his arms had just moments earlier. Held her and compelled her to be honest with him. With herself.

"I...I've given up fighting it." As difficult as it was for her to admit, the words, once said, made her spirits soar.

The pounding on the door echoed the pounding of her heart.

"Neesa! Are you all right?" Concern laced Claire's words.

"I'd better let her in." Neesa smoothed her T-shirt.

He stood. "I'd better get going."

Perhaps it was for the best. She needed time to absorb this new direction their relationship had taken. This new feeling of vitality and joy pumping through her veins.

He walked behind her to the door, which she opened on a wide-eyed Claire.

"Honey!" Her friend and neighbor burst through the doorway. "Are you sick? Sugah, you're flushed!" It was only after the first few seconds that Claire focused on Hank. "Well, I'll be—"

"Hank Whittaker, ma'am." Hank extended his hand.

Claire accepted it. "Claire English." She got a swoony look in her eyes as her gaze traveled the length and breadth of him.

Hank turned to Neesa. "Be in touch."

"Of course." She watched with undisguised longing as he strode to his truck. She might have stayed in the doorway watching his taillights fade into the night had Claire not pounced.

"And what were you doing that you couldn't answer the door?" Claire shook Neesa's shoulder playfully.

"We…I…Hank returned an agency folder I left at his ranch." Reluctantly she closed the door and felt his absence like a cold breeze.

"And you just fell to making out on the couch—"

"Claire!"

Claire's eyes widened. "You don't deny it!"

"Didn't we recently have a conversation about how absolutely impossible it was for me to consider anything but a professional relationship with Hank Whittaker?"

"Sure. I remember that conversation…but do you?"

"Come on in. I'll get your key."

"Forget the key! Tell me what changed between you and Mister Long, Tall and Hunky."

"Why in the world do you think anything's changed?" Normally she wasn't so obtuse with her best friend. But what had just happened between Hank and herself was so extraordinary that she didn't feel like sharing.

But still Claire persisted. "Why would I think anything's changed? Hah! Because that man looked at you as if he could purely gobble you up. Because your clothes are all rumpled, your hair's a mess and you're flushed beyond belief. I know postmake-out glow when I see it, sweetie!" Suddenly she covered her mouth with her hands. "I didn't interrupt *more,* did I?"

"No!" That wasn't exactly the truth. Who knew what might have happened on the sofa if Claire hadn't lost her key? "If you must know, he kissed me again." Now, there was sheer understatement.

Claire fairly danced with excitement. "And?"

"And I kissed him back."

"Oooh! What does all this mean?"

Neesa swatted Claire's shoulder. "It means I enjoy the man's company. It means I haven't had a date in ages. It means we might see each other outside work. That's all it means."

"So you feel comfortable with this?" Concern replaced mischief in Claire's eyes.

"As comfortable as I'll ever feel." Neesa grinned. "I don't envision a time when Hank Whittaker won't set me a little off balance."

"If you're fairly comfortable, you must have talked to him about your...situation."

Neesa stiffened.

Claire reached out and grasped both Neesa's hands. "You did tell him the only family you'll ever have is through adoption?"

Withdrawing her hands, Neesa headed for the kitchen where she kept the keys.

"Oh, Neesa, you didn't talk it over with him?"

"Why should I? Or, more specifically, why should I *now* when I don't even know if we'll ever progress beyond a couple of kisses?"

"Why? To save yourself hurt down the road."

Neesa grabbed Claire's house key from the rack above the sink. "You even said he wasn't Paul."

"Yeah, I said he wasn't Paul, but I also told you to be honest with him right from the start. Even a man not Paul needs a little time to cope with news this important."

"Not you, too!" Suddenly Neesa felt as if her best friend had turned on her.

"Aw, honey..." Claire slid her arm around Neesa's shoulders. "I said *important* not awful or fatal or insurmountable. You have to admit, infertility is something a couple should consider when looking at the future. With Paul and you it was different. You didn't know from the start."

No, but she'd thought their love strong enough to weather anything—for better or worse. She'd counted on love for keeps.

She'd been wrong.

Whistling up a storm, Hank entered the Cates County sheriff's office. He was too keyed up to head back to the ranch. Too full of thoughts of Neesa Little to attempt paperwork or sleep. Too…on top of the world. He might as well stop in to see his brother and spread around some of this good mood.

He spied Brett in his office, up to his elbows in department paperwork.

"Howdy." Hank leaned against the doorjamb and wished everyone could feel as fine as he did tonight.

Brett looked up, misery etched on his face. "Pushin' papers is going to be the death of me."

"Can I talk you into a beer?"

"In fact you can." Brett rose. "I'm not even on duty. I was just putting in some extra hours to get out from under this godawful mountain."

He called out to his deputy to say they'd be above, then led the way up a dark and rickety back staircase to his bachelor quarters over the sheriff's office.

Hank could not think of a drearier existence. But then his brother wasn't nesting.

Inside the one-room apartment, Brett opened the refrigerator. The contents consisted of four long-neck beers and a doughnut box. "What brings you to town so late?"

"Oh, this and that." Hank took the offered beer, then sat at one of the two straight-backed chairs next to a small kitchen table. The only other piece of furniture in the clean and spartan room was a single cot made up with military precision.

Sitting in the other chair, Brett narrowed his eyes. "'This and that' wouldn't have something to do with the pretty lady from Georgia's Waiting Children, now, would it?"

"Maybe." Hank grinned at the thought.

"Can't say as I disapprove." Brett reached across the table and clinked his beer bottle against Hank's. "You've turned into a regular hermit out at that ranch. You need to come into town once in a while for a good time."

"She's not just a good time." Hank bristled protectively.

Sitting up straighter in his chair, Brett cocked one eyebrow in a look of sheer cynicism. "You're not thinking of anything serious are you?"

"Why not?"

"For one, you just met her."

"Hey, Pa said he knew Ma was the one from the first moment he laid eyes on her."

"And died of a broken heart not two months after she passed."

"What's that supposed to mean?"

"Grand passion hurts. I'm only suggesting you use a little caution."

"Hell, my year-and-a-half engagement to Ellen was pretty damned cautious, and look where that got me." Hank slowly but surely began to burn. "I don't think time has anything to do with it. I think it's all about the people involved."

"Then let's talk about the people involved." Brett thunked his beer bottle down on the table top. "Have you forgotten you're a rancher?"

"The point being?"

"Granted, Miss Neesa Little is as pretty as they come. Pretty. Petite. Delicate and refined. She looks as suited to ranch life as a crystal chandelier at a barbecue."

Hank glared at his brother. "Looks can be deceiving."

"You want to settle down that badly."

"Hey, I'm not desperate." He grinned despite Brett's pessimism. "I just have a gut feeling that this lady's the one."

The more Hank grinned, the more Brett scowled.

"You do know the divorce statistics?" the sheriff asked none too gently. "You've seen the troubles cousin Evan and Cilla are going through?"

"She loves kids," Hank said to no one in particular.

Brett rolled his eyes. "She works for a placement agency. Before the signatures on the marriage license were dry, she'd have your ranch filled up with other people's kids. Other people's problems.''

"You always were a cantankerous coot. Now you're next to miserable.''

"Someone's got to think of the down-side possibilities.''

"Why?'' Hank smacked both hands, palm down, on the tabletop, rattling the beer bottles in the process. "Why can't I court Neesa Little with my brother's blessing? Why can't I have a houseful of my own kids and an equal number from Georgia's Waiting Children—''

Hank paused abruptly. That was the first time he'd had that notion.

Neesa seemed so worried that he would abandon Kids & Animals after he found the right woman, settled down, started his own family. But if Neesa were the right woman, why couldn't they have it all? Their own, plus. Heck, he'd always envisioned Whispering Pines hopping with a dozen or more rug rats.

He beamed despite his brother's storm cloud demeanor.

Brett groaned. "It's not enough Sam bit the dust in the matrimonial ring. Now you're getting all soft and gooey on me.''

The youngest Whittaker, Sam, had taken off for California. He'd written from Las Vegas where he'd married a showgirl and had never made it to the coast.

The thought of Neesa and his new plan made Hank magnanimous. He wouldn't let Brett pick a fight. But he couldn't resist a zinger. "You know, bro, a woman in your life might rub off some of those downright unpleasant rough edges.''

Shaking his head, Brett glared at his now empty beer bottle. "In my line of work, I need the rough edges.''

"Want to talk about it?''

"No.''

"Want to hear about Neesa?''

Brett harrumphed. "What ever happened to the magnificent Whittaker boys? We were going to be cowboys. Wild and free." He rose and smacked Hank's upper arm with the beer bottle. *"Free."*

"I can be in love and still be free."

Brett stood stock-still. "In love?"

The words out in the open kind of shocked Hank, too. But there was no taking them back. Especially not since they were true.

"Let me ask you this." Brett's voice was low and level, but his eyes held an intense need to know. "When you got to be an adult and you thought back on Pa and Ma's story, didn't you ever think that the sacrifices Pa made for love were too much to ask of a body?"

"Never." He hadn't. Not once. "That's the difference between you and me. You see the obstacles. I see the possibilities."

"You might get hurt."

"I've been hurt before and survived."

Brett shook his head. "I've gotta get back to that paperwork."

"Thanks for the beer." Hank rose from his chair. "And the words of encouragement."

"Hey, who always looked out for you after Ma and Pa passed?" Brett actually grinned. "You and Sam never did have the sense you were born with."

Hank followed his brother downstairs. While Brett hadn't managed to squelch his good mood, he'd brought up some points that had already given Hank cause for concern. Pa and Ma's love, although deep and abiding, hadn't come without pain. Too, Hank knew the statistical prognosis for a modern marriage. He himself had already been once burned, even before the "I do's." And on the surface Neesa didn't look like the kind of woman cut out for hardy ranch life.

But...

Despite the warnings, he wanted her.

Oh, how he wanted her.

Chapter Nine

Early Tuesday morning Neesa stood at the feed bins in Hank's barn, doling out bucketfuls of the various mixes to the Hadaway children, who in turn scurried about the barn, the barnyard and the outside pens, feeding Noah's ark.

A supreme sense of serenity cloaked her every movement.

With very little effort, she could picture herself the mother of these five. Could picture Hank as the father and Whispering Pines as their home. The dangerous thought took her breath away. She mentally made herself promise that she would never, ever utter that dream aloud to anyone. Not to Claire. Most certainly not to Hank. If she kept it tightly locked and silent within her heart, what harm could come of it?

Hidden as it was, her fantasy brought her great joy.

"A penny for your thoughts." Hank had come up unexpectedly behind her.

A delicious expectation ran through her in his presence. This morning was the first time they'd been together since Friday night. Although Hank was strictly proper with her in front of the children, there was a warmth, a boyish eagerness, a yearning to connect in the looks he sent her way. She responded in kind.

Whatever the future held, she wasn't going to deny the growing attraction she felt for him.

"I was just thinking," she said, smiling up at him, "what a wonderful day it is."

Martin came up beside them, filled his bucket from the bin of mash for the horses, scowled, then silently went about his chores.

"Not for that one," Hank said.

"Martin's not sure that this run of good luck will last. His surliness is his way of steeling himself against disappointment."

"I wish there was some way I could get him to trust me."

"Patience, Hank." She reached out tentatively and patted his arm, then flushed at his instant smile.

"Look what I brought you, Miss Neesa!" Skipping at Carlie's side, Rebecca held aloft a single daisy. "I found it growing next to the pigpen."

"Why, thank you!" Neesa knelt to accept the present. "I'd wear it in my buttonhole today…if I had a buttonhole." She looked forlornly at her T-shirt.

Hank reached for the daisy. "Here, let me." With a gentleness that tugged at her heart and a warmth of regard that made her pulse sing, he tucked the flower behind her ear. "Now doesn't she look the picture?" he asked the girls as he kept his unwavering gaze on Neesa.

The two girls giggled.

"Prettier than Amos with his daisy-chain necklace," Carlie said, her eye twinkling.

Hank stared wide-eyed. "You made my pig a flower necklace?"

"Yes, sir," the two replied in unison.

"He let you?"

"He even let Carlie scratch behind his ears."

"Did he now?" Hank rubbed his chin. "I'll have to let Willy know this. It might even help to change his opinion of old Amos."

Carlie looked over her shoulder before she spoke. "You know, Amos would get out of Miss Reba's garden a lot faster if Willy didn't holler at him."

Hank bent down, then whispered conspiratorially, "Do you have a better way to get him out of the garden?"

"Yup. Marshmallows." Carlie leaned so close to Hank that they were almost nose to nose. "I saw a pig on TV do tricks for marshmallows."

Hank chuckled. "Well, I'll have Miss Reba lay in a supply, and the next time Amos gets loose, we'll try out your theory."

Rebecca clapped her hands in anticipation.

"Now, don't you let Amos out on purpose," Hank cautioned. "Nor any of the other animals."

"Oh, no." Returning, Martin fairly threw his empty bucket on a nail on the wall. "We wouldn't want anything to happen to these precious mongrels." His mouth turned down in obvious contempt.

At the provocation, Hank remained calm. "Every living thing on Whispering Pines has worth, Martin. You included. I wouldn't want to tempt misfortune in any quarter."

The boy's gaze remained hard. "I promised Thomas I'd help Willy and him put up the tire swing."

"Afterward, maybe I could show you how to run the old truck. You're fifteen, do you have your driver's permit?"

"No." Martin looked at Hank as if the man were crazy. "What's the point? I live in a state home, in case you forgot." He turned sharply, then stomped out of the barn.

"Martin's mad," Rebecca whispered, popping her thumb in her mouth.

"Martin told us not to get too comfortable here," Carlie said softly.

"Martin's just afraid I'm going to pull up the welcome

mat." Staring after the teenager, Hank gently laid a hand on each girl's shoulder. "But I'm not. I promise."

Neesa's heart ached for the boy and swelled with pride at the man. She dearly wished she could find a way to smooth matters between the two. But time was her sole tool. If only Hank didn't get fed up with Martin's insolence—

She shut that thought down before it even reached fruition.

"Come on, girls," she said brightly, "Miss Reba and Nell need help in the garden."

"Yup," Hank added. "Beans for dinner, and we get to pick 'em."

"*We?*" This was the first Neesa had heard that Hank was going to give them any more time out of his schedule. "I don't expect you to neglect your business."

Lordy, but his grin was infectious. "Tucker's putting the logging horses through their paces, if that's what you're worried about. And as I told Martin, everything on a ranch is important. I promised Reba I'd turn her garden compost heap, repair the rabbit fence. Better to do it now when I've got bean pickers for company."

"Let's go, Miss Neesa!" Rebecca tugged on Neesa's jeans.

"Don't dawdle, Miss Neesa," Hank drawled, slipping his hand in hers. "I can't wait to see the three of you in Reba's sun hats."

Neesa harrumphed softly. "It'll crush my daisy." She had no complaints, however, about holding hands.

With Neesa's hand in his, Hank felt as if nothing could go wrong today. Even Martin's jaded outlook and emotional wall would have to give way eventually under the high spirits of the others. Hank counted as well on Whispering Pines to work its magic.

He breathed deeply of the clean, pine-scented air. He loved the land. He loved the honest, hard work on the

ranch. He loved the laughter of children. And now he loved
Miss Neesa Little.

He flashed a grin in her direction and was rewarded when
she unselfconsciously beamed a smile right back at him.

Oh, things had changed since Friday night. They'd both
taken that scary first step toward exploring a relationship.
And nothing could go wrong. He felt it in his bones.

"Hank?" Carlie's sweet, high voice broke into his
thoughts. "Thomas said Tucker promised if they can get
Gizmo's leg better, Tucker'll teach Thomas how to train
him to a cart. Can we all ride in it if he does?"

He ruffled her sun-warm hair. "You sure can." It was
wonderful to hear these children planning for the future. It
felt good to be a part of their plans if only part-time.

"Miss Reba!" Neesa called out happily. "Here come
your bean pickers."

"Just in time." Reba held up three old-fashioned sun
bonnets. "You each have to put one of these on. Ranch
sunscreen."

"I want the pink one!" Rebecca held out her hand for
a faded red gingham prairie bonnet.

Carlie helped her little sister tie the bonnet's ribbons,
then took a floppy blue cotton hat with an enormous silk
sunflower on the brim for herself. That left a wide-brimmed
straw which Hank took from Reba before Neesa could.

He turned to her, then slowly lowered the old hat over
her blond hair. As with the daisy earlier, it was just an
excuse to touch her. To look at her a little longer. To eke
out a tiny island of privacy in a very public day.

She held his gaze for a long time as if she understood.

Nell popped up from where she'd been kneeling in the
warm red earth. "Don't we look like a garden full of flowers!"

"Long-stemmed beauties," Hank agreed, his heart full
to overflowing.

Reba whacked his chest unceremoniously in passing.
"Sweet talk will get you nowhere. Either pick beans, turn

the compost, or get back to work with your horses. Loafing will find you with no dinner.''

"And I know for certain there's chocolate cream pie for dessert." Nell, in the few short hours she'd spent on Whispering Pines, looked like a new girl. Fresh-faced and smiling.

"Where are the beans?" Rebecca asked.

"Hiding," Nell replied. "It's like a treasure hunt. Come see."

Hank lingered a moment longer, watching the women and girls move about the kitchen garden. He could very easily get used to this diversion. This feminine presence on his ranch.

"Still not working?" Neesa flashed him a mock-horrified look from under the wide brim of her straw hat. "Dibs on Hank's slice of chocolate cream pie!" she called out to the others.

"I'm working! I'm working!" Holding up his hands in surrender, Hank backed toward the compost heap. You couldn't tell him there was anything wrong with this new life.

As the all-female crew picked fresh produce for the midday meal, Hank set about spading the compost heap with a vengeance, ideas percolating in his brain. He'd have to discuss them with Neesa later. He wondered if it would do the Hadaway kids good to interact with other children on the ranch. He was thinking specifically about Chris and Casey. His little cousins could show the Hadaways the meaning of all-out fun, and the Hadaways could show the Russells the benefits of sibling loyalty. Maybe he'd organize a picnic or a barbecue. A big family affair—

A shriek sliced the air.

He looked up to see that pandemonium had erupted in the garden. As Reba hustled the Hadaway girls toward the house, Neesa stood frantically swatting the air with her straw hat.

Great Scott, he thought. Hornets. She'd only get stung, agitating them so.

Without thinking twice, Hank leaped over the garden's picket fence. "Neesa! Drop the hat!"

She didn't seem to hear him. Seemed too intent upon whacking the hornets away from her, which only made the insects angrier.

Oblivious to the prospect of getting stung himself, he grasped the straw hat, then flung it across the rows of vegetables. "Be still, Neesa," he ordered as calmly as possible, while he scooped her into his arms and carried her through the garden, then across the small flagstone area into the kitchen. He had a cousin who'd died of a hornet sting. Time was of the essence.

He noticed a growing red bump at the corner of her mouth. "Have you ever been stung before?"

"Yes...last year...at the agency picnic."

"Any abnormal effects?"

"My co-workers teased me for a week." She looked up at him woefully. "I was stung on my behind."

Relief coursed through him as he lowered her to a kitchen chair.

Reba bustled through the kitchen, a can of insecticide in her hand. "The girls are settled in the dining room, snapping beans. The baking soda's in the cupboard. I'm going to spray the nest. It was in the ground. Right at the end of my row of lettuce. The poor love stepped on it."

The screen door banged behind her retreating form.

"Owwww!" Neesa gingerly touched the sting next to her mouth. "What a fool I've been."

"Now why would you say that?" Having retrieved the baking soda from the cupboard, Hank made a paste with a little water in a saucer. Realizing that Neesa wasn't in any real danger, his heartbeat had returned to normal.

"Because I'm so totally inept on this ranch. I can't seem to catch the rhythm. Like a fish out of water. I don't belong here."

He didn't like the self-condemning tone in her voice. Earlier he'd felt an overwhelming protectiveness toward her physical well-being. Now he felt the same about her emotional outlook. "Anyone can step on an in-ground hive. You don't expect one underfoot."

"It's not just the hornets." Discovering another sting on the back of one wrist, she examined it intently.

He knelt before her with the baking soda paste. "Here. Let me." He took her hand in his. Turned it over. Applied the paste to the sting. "Why else are you beating yourself up?"

"You do remember the first time I set foot on your ranch?"

How could he ever forget?

"I ripped my blouse, broke my shoe heel and twisted my ankle."

"If I remember correctly, Bowser had you under siege." He turned his attention to the sting next to her mouth. Such a pretty mouth. So kissable. He dabbed a bit of paste on the reddened area and tried not to daydream about her kisses. "How's that feel?"

"The bite's going out of the sting."

"Good. Neither sting looks abnormal. Is your breathing okay?"

"Yes. Fine."

He ran his fingers up and down her arms and along her neck. "I don't see any rashes or unusual skin coloring." He smiled at her. "The doc declares you'll survive. This time with your dignity intact." He cast his gaze toward her well-rounded bottom.

She rolled her eyes. "And for such a foolish thing I've upset the girls."

"I'll check. You sit tight." He rose, then went to the dining room door.

Nell, Carlie and Rebecca were seated around the big old oak table, snapping beans, talking in hushed whispers. Rebecca was chewing on a string bean as if it were a licorice stick.

"You girls okay?" he asked.

Nell looked up. "Is Miss Neesa?"

"Yup. She looks a little splotchy with baking soda paste on her though." He grinned reassuringly.

"Miss Reba said you'd know just what to do." Nell's eyes held a trust that was nothing less than awe inspiring.

"If you don't mind, I have something to discuss with Miss Neesa in the kitchen. Afterward she'll join you."

"Take your time." Nell sat up straighter. "Miss Reba put me in charge."

Hank sent the three a wink before returning to the kitchen.

"All set in there." He pulled a wooden chair up close to Neesa. "Now, want to tell me what put the idea in your head that you don't belong on this ranch?"

Although more than once he'd thought the very same, he'd fought the idea because he wanted her so much. At this point in his plans for the two of them, he wasn't about to let her start fortifying his earlier pessimistic thoughts.

She waved him away. "They're just little insecurities." She started to rise. "We really should get back to the children."

He put his hand on her arm to stay her. "The children are fine. All five of them." He looked deep into her eyes. "I want to know why you said you feel uncomfortable on this ranch."

Neesa felt the gentle pressure of his hand on her arm and the much more intense pressure of his regard, forcing her back in her seat. She regretted having spoken so rashly. It wasn't like her to engage her tongue before her brain. In the few instances she ever had, she'd revealed more of herself than she'd intended. That was the case now.

"I didn't say I was uncomfortable," she replied carefully.

"You said you felt like a fish out of water."

"I've never been a country girl." She took a deep breath. "I was born and raised in the suburbs."

"So?"

"So I'm supposed to be the leader in this Kids & Animals program, and I know as little—if not less—about ranch life than the kids do."

"Are you saying you feel like a fraud?" He leaned forward and brushed a wisp of hair behind her ear. "If so, I'd say your enthusiasm has made up for any lack of specific knowledge."

Bless his heart. He was performing verbal cartwheels to put her at ease.

"I should have been more aware of my surroundings. What if one of the girls had been stung?"

"They weren't."

"I never knew hornets could make nests in the ground."

"Now you do." He took her hand in his. "And so do the girls. It was a learning experience. Wasn't that what you brought the Hadaways to my ranch for?"

She smiled despite the jumble of still-unexplained feelings within her. "I'm supposed to be in charge of activities. But if I'm ignorant and you always have to step in to save me, how are you going to get any work done on Tuesdays and Fridays?"

"That's why I have Willy and Tucker and Reba."

"But Reba's cleaning up after my hornet disaster, and Willy's making a tire swing with Martin, and Tucker's talking with Thomas about training a mule to pull a cart. You tell me what regular ranch work you've accomplished this morning."

His eyes sparkled as he grinned at her and stroked the palm of her hand. "So I rearrange my schedule for Tuesdays and Fridays and I put in a little extra time before and after the Hadaways are here. So that should make you feel inept?" He reached out and touched the tip of her nose with his finger. "You don't like my company?"

His gentle touch and his soul-searching gaze left her tongue-tied.

"Because I like yours just fine," he added huskily. "And, besides, I promised myself that today nothing could go wrong."

"A wild woman in your veggie patch doesn't count?"

"Not if she doesn't let it." He turned her hand palm up, then placed a soft, warm kiss right in the center.

Neesa looked over the top of Hank's lowered head to see Martin glowering at them through the screen of the kitchen door. When her gaze met his, the teenager quickly turned and disappeared. A cold shiver ran down her spine.

"Hank, Martin was just here. At the door. He saw us like this."

Hank slowly released her hand, then stood. "Do you want me to talk to him?"

"No." She rose, too. "I will. Then there'll be less of that male posturing he likes to throw your way."

Hank reached out to touch her cheek. "There was nothing wrong with what he saw."

Neesa felt heat flush her face. "You and I know that. I don't know what Martin thinks he saw, however." She turned to follow Martin.

She found him leaning against the paddock, watching Tucker exercise the enormous draft horses. "Martin, I'd like to talk to you."

He didn't look at her. His body language said, Go away. "You sweet on Hank?" The blunt question couldn't hide his animosity.

"Yes, I am." She figured Martin deserved honesty at the very least.

"Has he asked you to marry him?"

"No!" She reached out and laid her hand upon the boy's shoulder until he turned to look at her. Confusion seemed to reign in his eyes. "We haven't even had what you'd call a date. We just like each other. A lot. We're getting to know each other."

"For sure he'll want to marry you."

"And would that be so awful?"

Martin turned away from her. Squinted out over the paddock again. It almost seemed as if he were fighting tears. "You two don't owe us Hadaways anything."

"Oh, yes, we do!"

He cut her a sidelong glance but said nothing.

"We owe you respect for your feelings and honesty as to our intentions." She leaned a little. Tried and failed to make eye contact. "We intend to make a go of Kids & Animals. Hank himself promised your sisters he wouldn't pull up the welcome mat. I think that's how he put it."

"Yeah? He might think twice about that when he has a family of his own. Then the five of us would just be in the way." He whirled to face her. "You're not tied to us by blood." He smeared the back of his hand over his eyes. "Willy told me I should wash up for dinner. I'll do it at the pump."

Neesa sighed deeply. There had been so much impermanence in that boy's life that he just didn't dare hope. Unfortunately, he'd learned early that nothing is for keeps, and so he expected rejection sooner or later.

Well, she for one was determined to make it later if ever. With a resolute stride she headed for the kitchen to see if she could help Reba and the girls with the midday meal.

Hank sat at his desk and stared at the appointment calendar in front of him. He'd come into his office to spend a few minutes before the dinner bell to clarifying some business matters. In his preoccupation with Neesa and the Hadaways he'd completely forgotten that he had a one-week logging contract up in the northeast corner of the state starting tomorrow.

He hated to leave. His absence would mean he'd miss Friday and next Tuesday with the Hadaways and Wednesday evening with Neesa. Not to mention a possible weekend with Neesa if he could convince her they should openly date.

He didn't see why they shouldn't. They were both adults, free and independent. Fully capable of keeping their professional and their personal relationships—the cool and the hot—separate. Moreover, dealing with the Hadaways would get the two of them used to working as a team on family matters.

Oh, family mattered.

Sitting forward at his desk, he stared out the window at the rolling expanse of pasture and forest. How he loved this land. It was strange how the Hadaways—no blood relations—had brought a new vitality, a new buzz of activity to the ranch. Hank shook his head. *Buzz* certainly was an appropriate choice of word.

Earlier Neesa had worried that she'd brought ineptitude and confusion into his schedule. She hadn't. She'd brought life.

When Pa and Ma were alive and running Whispering Pines—back when Hank, Brett and Sam were boys—not only did the ranch hum with hard work, but more often than not it whooped with puerile hijinks. Those were good times.

The land had always meant the most to Hank. That's why he'd inherited the ranch. He'd always seen himself as Gary Cooper. Brett, although he could get into as much trouble as the next, had a streak in him that cried out for justice. Ma had nicknamed him Wyatt Earp. And Sam...well, Sam had been mischief personified. He'd beg Pa to tell and retell tales of his favorite mythical hero, Pecos Bill. When the brothers went their separate ways, however, a quiet had settled over Whispering Pines.

Now, with the advent of the Hadaways, Hank recognized the quiet as unnatural. The ranch needed laughter and tire swings and scrapes and bumps and even the difficult struggles of a teenage boy trying to reach manhood.

Rising to wash up for the noonday meal, Hank rubbed

the back of his neck. He wished that Martin and he could reach accord. He wished Neesa would trust him more when it came to Martin. He could understand her protectiveness, but the times when she and he were at cross purposes about the welfare of the teenager troubled him. Maybe matters would ride easier when they had their own family—

Tucker burst into the room. "Martin's let the animals loose!"

"How could that be?"

"One minute we were all washing up for dinner, the next minute it was just Willy, Thomas and me. We thought Martin had headed for the house."

Out of the corner of one eye, Hank saw the flash of pot-bellied porker in Reba's garden. "Noah's ark?"

"All of it. And the two Percherons I was working with in the paddock."

"Damn!" The Percherons were valuable animals. An integral part of his bread and butter. "We'd better get to work. Where's the boy?"

"Reba saw him streakin' off toward the high pasture."

Smacking his Stetson on his head, Hank brushed past Tucker. "Whoever inherits the Hadaways might just need his head examined." He ran right into Neesa, and instantly regretted his thoughtless oath.

It was something an irate father might utter when his son has done something stupid. But because Hank wasn't Martin's father, his remark sounded cruel.

And the angry look in Neesa's eyes said she'd heard every word of it.

"We need to find Martin," she said.

"We need to corral my Percherons."

"The two horses mean more than one boy?"

"No." He didn't need this delay, but it was important he make things clear between them. "I think I know why Martin did this. And I know he won't run off far and leave his brother and sisters to take the blame. Horses, on the other hand, don't have ulterior motives. They could be in the next county while we stand arguing.''

Tucker stepped forward. ''Willy and I'll see to the horses. Reba's organized the other kids to round up Noah's ark. You two see to Martin.''

''I'll take care of Martin.'' Neesa's whole body was stiff with determination.

''I'm not being shut out this time.'' Hank grasped her elbow and propelled her down the hallway. ''You can act as referee, but this beef is between Martin and me.''

''I don't want you hurting him.''

He whirled to face her. ''Do you think I'd lay a hand on the boy?''

''Emotionally,'' she said. ''I don't want you to hurt him emotionally.''

''He needs the respect of discipline.''

''He needs understanding.''

''I understand him.''

''You do?'' Surprise widened her blue eyes.

''Come on. I'm not an ogre. We can talk as we walk. If my hunch plays out, we have a hike.''

Leaving the ranch house by the back, they headed up into the high pasture.

''What do you mean you understand him?'' Neesa asked.

''I talked about Martin with my brother Brett. As sheriff, he handles difficult kids. I thought maybe Martin had a crush on you. Was jealous of me.''

''I never imagined!''

''Well, Brett thinks it's more likely Martin sees you and me as an item. Sees far enough down the road to where you and I might marry. Might start a family with our own kids.''

''Then the Hadaways would be expendable.''

''Exactly.''

''But that's so far from the truth that it's—''

''Remember, we're dealing with a teenage mind here. And this is no ordinary teenager. He's the head of the Hadaways. Blood loyalty demands he protect his siblings from any occurrence he sees as a threat.''

"Oh, dear." She raised her hand to her mouth. "He saw us in the kitchen. Then he asked me afterward if we were going to get married.''

"If I know teenage boys like I think I do, Martin has been waiting for the ax to fall. And sometimes the wait seems worse than anything that might happen. I think that, rather than sit back and worry, he precipitated the inevitable. He wants to see how mad I can get. He wants to see how disposable he and his family are in my estimation.''

"How mad are you?"

"Damn mad. He knew full well what those Percherons mean.''

"But he's a boy, Hank!"

"Even boys need to face up to the consequences of their actions.''

"What are you going to do?"

"He and I are going to reach an understanding."

"Please, think of the others."

"I am thinking of the others. If I let Martin get away with this, what kind of respect could I ask of him or the others? What kind of a father would I be?''

Her gasp came short and sweet. "You're not their father.''

No, he wasn't. Chalk that slip up to wishful thinking.

"This is about trust, Neesa. Trust between the kids and me. Trust between you and me." He stared long and hard at her. "Do you trust me?''

She answered him with an anguished look and silence.

Chapter Ten

Neesa never had answered Hank on that matter of trust between them. Before she'd been able to reply to his question, he'd spotted Martin in the branches of a spreading oak tree, the same one the teenager had refused to explore on his first visit to Whispering Pines. The tree was far enough away from the ranch so that the boy had delayed the inevitable, but close enough that he'd been able to keep an eye on the activity and his brother and sisters below.

Martin now stood before Hank's desk in the ranch office. Hank, his fingers tented before him, his midnight dark eyes unreadable, sat behind the desk, his body stiff with suppressed anger. With the uncomfortable feeling that they were in a courtroom, Neesa sat in a chair not far from Martin.

Did she trust Hank?

She couldn't honestly say yes or no. She hadn't known him long enough. Perhaps this incident today was a timely reminder not to go falling head over heels in love with a stranger.

Hank's expression certainly was not his usual. His jaw

set, his gaze flinty, he appeared every inch the strict authoritarian. But how just would his authority prove?

Neesa worried that, despite his promise to the girls, Hank might have come to the end of his patience where this pilot program was concerned.

"Martin." Hank's voice rumbled, low and controlled. "Why did you let the animals loose?"

His gaze focused on the wall above Hank's head, Martin remained shrouded in insolent silence.

Although Neesa's heart went out to the teenager, Hank was right about one thing: they would be doing Martin no favors by allowing irresponsible behavior. She only wished she knew what Hank considered proper discipline. For that reason she'd insisted on being present while the man and the boy worked matters out.

Hank tried again. "I'm assuming that you specifically let the Percherons loose to get at me. To get my attention perhaps. Am I right?"

Martin continued to glower at the wall. "Why don't you send us all back to the home and get it over with?"

"Is that what you think I'm going to do?"

"Sooner or later." The teenager hazarded a glance at Hank.

"And you thought by acting out you'd make me do it sooner? Get it over with?"

"The younger ones are settling in here too fast. Getting too attached. They don't realize all good things gotta end. And for us Hadaways they always end as fast as they begin."

Neesa looked at Hank. The light in his eyes seemed to say that he'd also heard Martin refer obliquely to the Whispering Pines experience as a "good thing." Maybe there was hope after all.

"Martin, have you enjoyed your time at the ranch?" Hank leaned forward on his elbows. His voice was gruff, but the stiffness had gone out of his posture. "I'm talking about you, now. Not the others."

The boy had returned his gaze to the wall. He didn't answer.

"Have we treated you well?" Hank rose, came round the desk, then sat on the edge, only a very short distance from Martin. "Willy. Tucker. Miss Reba. Miss Neesa. Me. Have we treated you with respect?"

Martin's lower lip trembled.

Neesa held her breath. It seemed that Hank had begun to do what countless social workers and counselors had failed to do: he'd begun to get through to a proud and emotionally besieged boy.

"I respect you, Martin." Hank's voice turned quiet. "I do. I respect you for the care you take of your brother and your sisters. I respect your family loyalty. Your strength. Is it so crazy I should want a little respect from you?"

Martin looked at the floor. A fat tear rolled down his cheek to plop in a dark spot on his boot. "I screwed up," he said so softly his words were almost inaudible.

Reaching out, Hank laid a hand on the teenager's shoulder. "It takes a man to admit that. Now, are you man enough to take your punishment?"

"Hank—" Concerned that Martin had been put through enough, Neesa half rose out of her seat, but Hank cut her off with a look.

"Martin, you've caused my crew an afternoon of work they never should have had to do. You upset your brother and sisters. You disrespected me and my property. Can you think of a fitting punishment?"

Martin shook his head.

Neesa felt as if her entire body were stuck with pins and needles. She didn't see where Hank was taking this. Could he possibly want to break the boy's spirit? Wariness engulfed her while she prepared to intervene at any moment.

"Perhaps," Hank went on, "you didn't understand the seriousness of your actions because you don't yet know the ins and outs of ranch life. What I do for a living. How I provide for me and my workers. How important the Percherons are to my business. Could that be the case?''

Martin nodded slowly.

''Then maybe you need to spend more time at Whispering Pines. Maybe you can make up for what you did this afternoon by helping out every day instead of just Tuesdays and Fridays. Real man's work so you'll know what I'm up against. For, say, a month.''

''Every day for a month! I don't know if the home officials will agree!'' Neesa exclaimed at the same time she noticed a flicker of interest in Martin's eyes.

''Oh, we'd have to make sure it was acceptable all around.'' Maintaining his stern demeanor, Hank folded his arms across his chest. ''Maybe after a month, we could talk about a paycheck.''

Sudden outrage colored Martin's features. ''You want them to pay you to put up with me?''

Hank actually chuckled. ''I was thinking more that I would pay you for your work.''

''Like a job?'' The teenager's eyes grew enormous.

''A summer job. You still have school in the fall.''

Neesa began to see Hank's plan, and her heart swelled with emotion at the man's understanding and generosity. He was holding the boy accountable for his actions at the same time he was demonstrating that his own involvement in Kids & Animals was not a fleeting notion. He was showing his authority as head of the ranch while showing Martin that the teenager was valued.

Hank had asked her to trust him. He was quickly proving himself worthy of that trust.

''Can I, Miss Neesa?'' Longing sparked in Martin's eyes.

''We'll have to go through channels.'' She smiled. ''But I think it can be arranged.''

Martin's expression suddenly soured. ''What about the others? What about Nell, Thomas, Carlie and Rebecca? They need me around.''

''Yeah, they do,'' Hank agreed. ''But they also need to

develop the strength and independence of their big brother. I'm not talking about working you from dawn to dusk. You'll still see your family."

Martin scowled. "I'll think it over."

"Well, consider this on top of everything else. I need help that can run the tractor and the old truck. You'd have to get your driver's permit."

"Impossible." The boy's shoulders drooped.

"Impossible?" Hank scratched his chin. "Now, that's a word I purely dislike. You'd have to call the motor vehicles department to find out the steps you go through, but Miss Neesa and I would help you after that."

"You would?" Martin looked from Neesa to Hank.

"I can say without a doubt that we would." Neesa beamed her approval at Hank.

"I'll still have to think about it." The boy's features grew sober again. "I have to think of the others."

"You think about it," Hank said as he walked to the office's closed door. "But if you don't accept these terms, we still have to come to agreement on how you're going to pay me back for the missed time and effort this afternoon."

"I realize that...sir." Martin looked Hank right in the eye.

"One more thing before we go eat Miss Reba's now-cold dinner." Hank paused before opening the door. "There comes a time when brothers and sisters, no matter how close, have to chart their own course in life. You won't ever lose the closeness. Believe me. I have brothers. I know."

When Hank opened the door, Reba, Willy and four Hadaways nearly fell into the room.

At that very moment, her heart filled to overflowing with hope, Neesa could have kissed Hank.

Hank deliberated on where to place the candles—on the old oak dining room table or on the veranda picnic table.

He wanted tonight's late supper with Neesa to be as special as their day had been.

They'd faced more than a few obstacles—Martin's sabotage ranking right at the top of the list—and had come out a team.

Hank knew how difficult it had been for Neesa to allow him the opportunity to straighten things out between himself and the teenager. If she'd interrupted this time, Martin would know he held a divisive power. Matters would have only gotten testier. But Neesa had trusted Hank—although reluctantly if her body language could be believed. And the end result had felt like family.

He'd asked her to come back tonight, ostensibly to make up for the Wednesday planning session they would miss because of his out-of-town contract. In reality, he planned to begin the seduction.

Hearing her car's tires on the gravel outside, he quickly decided on an intimate dinner for two in the old-fashioned dining room. Despite the day's roller-coaster ride, in the end nothing had gone wrong if you put the emphasis on happy endings. He vowed to keep the record intact with this romantic interlude.

"Hello?" Her clear sweet voice wafted through the house.

He plunked the candlesticks down on the dining room table, then eagerly went to meet her.

She stood on the veranda, looking in through the screen door. And was she ever a vision, wearing a tiny little shift of a dress that hugged her curves and accented her femininity. A sophisticated scent preceded her, sending his senses into overdrive. She smiled when she saw him and lit up his hopes and dreams.

"Hey." He opened the door for her.

She paused, then stood on tiptoe to plant a soft kiss on his cheek. "I trust you," she whispered.

Saints alive. If that didn't set the tone for the evening.

Slipping his arm around her waist, he drew her close. "Care to skip supper?"

"No." A sexy mischief sparkled in her eyes. "Something tells me I'm going to need my strength."

He kissed her then with a hunger he'd never before felt. His pulse raced with the taste of her. With the feel of her pressed against him, her fingers entwined in his hair. She made him hot and impatient.

"Whoa, cowboy!" She pulled away. Breathless but laughing nonetheless. "Are you trying to kiss me into next week?"

"Yup." He grinned down at her nestled in the circle of his arms. "I'll be gone that long."

"I'll miss you."

That admission gave him great satisfaction. "So tonight's a going away party as well as a celebration."

"And you said it was a planning session."

He nuzzled her neck. "Oh, I have plans...."

"I like the sound of plans." She cupped his face in her hands so that he had to look directly into her eyes. "With you."

The thready quality of her words and the honest intensity of her gaze made desire rise deep within him. "Long-range plans."

Her regard wavered. "One step at a time."

"First step...kisses."

She placed a finger lightly on his lips. "First step...supper." The sparkle quickly returned to her eyes.

As much as his body ached for her, he could wait. He was convinced they had a lifetime to explore desire and a host of other emotions he felt in her presence.

"Supper," he agreed, taking her hand in his. "Reba left a feast, and Willy donated a bottle of his dandelion wine."

"Is it drinkable?"

"Far too drinkable if you ask me."

"Thanks for the warning." She squeezed his hand and looked up at him through thick lashes. "I'll take it slowly."

Her words slithered over him in heady double meaning. Slow with Neesa would be heaven. Slow and hot and lasting. Rumpled sheets and long nights. Slick bodies and hunger sated....

Hard arousal reminded him to cool it or they'd never make it to the table.

"Can I help you?"

Could she help him? He could think of a hundred bodily ways. He turned to pull her into his arms once more.

"With supper, I mean." She grinned up at him wickedly as her eyes maintained an angelic innocence.

"You tempt a man sorely, Miss Neesa Little." He drank in the sight of her. His for the evening. With luck, his for the future.

She lowered her gaze. With her index finger she traced a lazy circle around his shirt button. "I'm still a little in awe of this chemistry between us."

"In awe," he repeated, tilting her chin up. "Not afraid?"

"I'm going to try to be as brave with you as you were with Martin today."

What an odd answer.

"Why do you say I was brave with Martin?" He pussyfooted around the question of her bravery with himself.

"You had to walk an emotional highwire today. Without a safety net. You had to preserve your authority while preserving Martin's dignity, as well. Some men wouldn't have undertaken such a sensitive task. Not with a boy who wasn't their son."

"Just because he isn't my son doesn't mean I shouldn't try to show him right from wrong."

Neesa looked long and hard at Hank. Although she'd told him just now that she trusted him, there was a question nagging at the back of her mind since Martin had let the animals loose. She took a deep breath, then decided to ask it and clear the air.

"Earlier you said that the couple who considered adopting the Hadaways should have their heads examined—"

"It was reflex, Neesa. Something my Pa would've said on any number of occasions when Brett, Sam or I gave him a splitting headache."

"You didn't mean it?"

"No." He smiled down at her, and his smile was tender. "I hope from the bottom of my heart that a kindhearted couple will see the Hadaways as special. Will welcome them into their home. Until then, I'll sponsor Kids & Animals...and keep the aspirin handy."

His gentle words only partly comforted her. He had admitted the Hadaways were special. He'd declared his commitment to Kids & Animals. But he'd said nothing about even the remotest possibility of taking the five children into his own home full-time.

How could she have asked for any more than he'd already given? His participation in and enthusiasm for the pilot program had exceeded her initial expectations. He'd been honest with her all along. He would help her, yes, but he wanted a family *of his own*. A biological dynasty.

And tonight he was showing signs of wanting to establish that dynasty with her.

She felt a trickle of fear run down her spine. If she were as brave with him as she said she would be, she'd tell him now about her infertility. But a desire to take pleasure in the moment made cowardice win out.

"I'm famished," she said with false heartiness. "What can I do to hurry supper?"

"You can set the table." His eyes held unspoken questions. Could he really see to the bottom of her soul? To the things she'd left unsaid? "I was running late because I had to get my travel supplies in order."

Ah, yes. He was leaving tomorrow and would be gone for the week. Perhaps that was just as well. Perhaps absence would place a little perspective on matters of the heart.

"Shall I use the dishes from the kitchen?" It helped to calm her, having something ordinary to do.

"No. Use the good stuff in the dining room highboy. My

ma's.'' He kissed her lightly on the mouth. ''Tonight's special.''

It felt odd—and at the same time natural—to be moving through his house. Touching his things. Working side by side to put an evening meal on the table. As if they belonged together as a couple.

A childless couple they would have to be.

Neesa held back tears as she lifted the quaint china from the highboy. She wanted Hank and knew she shouldn't.

By the time she'd set the table and he'd placed the food on it, she'd regained her composure. The dandelion wine helped. They ate and talked about Hank's upcoming week. About the horses and the glories of the north Georgia mountains. About the blessing of being able to work out-of-doors. About the terrific feeling of independence self-employment brought. In fact, they talked about everything except what lay heavy on Neesa's heart: the inner truth.

Her infertility.

Having come this far, having experienced joy and hope and passion in only a short time with Hank, she didn't want to risk it all with the truth. She'd said she trusted him. She didn't, however, know if she could trust his reaction to this one last secret.

''You've hardly touched your food.'' His words broke into her thoughts. ''I'll be the one Reba scolds.''

''It's been a pretty full day. The excitement's tired me, I'm afraid.''

''Come on.'' He rose from the table. ''I know what you need.''

''But the dishes—''

''I'll do them later.''

''You won't leave them for Reba—''

''No way.'' He grinned. ''The woman purely intimidates me.''

Neesa couldn't imagine anything intimidating this big, strapping cowboy.

He led her to the living room. "Kick off your sandals," he instructed, "then lie back on the sofa cushions."

"Don't tell me we're going to watch Sports Center."

"What kind of a Neanderthal do you take me for?" He feigned hurt.

Warily, she kicked off her sandals, then sat on the end of the sofa.

He cocked his head. "I said lie back."

She leaned.

"Farther."

She let her shoulders touch the cushions.

"Farther." His voice oozed a sexy authority.

"Why?"

"Are all women this suspicious?" Sitting on the sofa, he scooped both her feet into his lap, causing her to recline fully. "You said you trusted me."

The look of pure desire he cast over the length of her was not to be trusted. Oh, no. Not at all.

"You said you were tired." He began to massage her feet. "I thought I'd put you more in a relaxed frame of mind." His massage was deep and pleasurable. "More...in the mood."

Yes, his touch definitely put her in the mood.

Continuing his rhythmic massage, he slid his hands under her calves. She felt unduly warm as she yielded to this sweet stroking. Her thoughts turned from the impossible to the possible. To the probable. To the inevitable. As if mesmerized, she watched him caress her body with his hands as well as with his dark gaze, longing evident in his eyes and in the tips of his fingers. A lovely primal song had begun in the very depths of her body.

"You are so beautiful," he murmured. His hands slid further up her body like a rising tide about to sweep her away.

Why was it so hard to think when he touched her?

He murmured her name as he lowered himself to lie beside her. He cradled her head against his shoulder. Ran his fingers over her cheek. Down her neck. Around the curve of her breast. "It seems like I've wanted you forever."

"How could that be?" she asked, tracing the outline of his mouth. "It hasn't even been two weeks since we met."

"Some things are meant to be." He lowered his mouth to hers.

It felt as if she would dissolve in his slow, sensuous kiss.

It seemed as if her body molded perfectly to his.

As his tongue swept hers, she forgot everything but the moment in the safety of his arms. He was hers. At least for now.

She let her hands explore his body. The planes of his handsome face. The warmth of his well-muscled chest. The lean strength of his hips. And even the hardness of his arousal straining tight-fitting jeans.

She felt no fear. Only joy coupled with an unspeakable yearning.

He planted kisses along the rim of her jaw. Little nips. Flicks of his tongue. He cupped her breast in his big hand. Rubbed her nipple to exquisite attention with the pad of his thumb. Then he pulled her tighter to him. Up against the length of him. Up against his hardness.

Her thoughts went muzzy wanting him. She struggled to maintain a sense of self.

"Hank..."

"Mmm?" He drew back, his smile crooked and lazy, his hooded gaze filled with an arresting sensuality. His hand lay possessively on her breast.

"Let me catch my breath. I—"

"It's okay." He gazed at her with the utmost tenderness. "I'll just look at you awhile."

That was dangerous, too. Why, just a look from him could make her forget her name. She inhaled sharply and tried to keep her wits about her.

"What do you see when you look at me?" she asked.

"The future."

It was such a straightforward answer it shook her equilibrium.

"Stay with me the night," he urged, unsettling her further.

Oh, how she wanted to. "I can't...I mean...I didn't come prepared." Nothing had prepared her for Hank.

"I have protection if that's what you're talking about...."

No! How could he know she didn't need protection? Not from pregnancy at least.

"Although..." He nuzzled her neck. "I wouldn't mind if...well, you have to know by now that I would purely love to hold a baby born of our lovemaking. She would have your blue eyes—"

"No!" The fantasy shattered, Neesa sat bolt upright. "I can't let this go on!"

Although confusion reigned in Hank's steady gaze, he released her.

She perched on the edge of the sofa, her back to him. "There is something about me you should know."

He sat up beside her. "What is it?" Worry lined those three words.

"It's not that I didn't want to be honest with you. I did. But this isn't something you bring up in casual conversation. And you have to admit our relationship hasn't followed the normal progression—"

"Just tell me, Neesa." He touched her chin, turning her to face him.

She backed away from his touch, stood, then paced the hardwood floor. Images of Paul—his disgust at her deficiency—crowded her thoughts, making disclosure the hardest thing she'd had to do in a long, long time.

"What the hell is so wrong that you can't love me?" The muscle in Hank's jaw twitched. His eyes had gone almost black.

She whirled to face him. "I can't have your babies."

"I don't understand."

"I'm infertile. That's why Paul left me." There. It was out in the open. And being free and clear, it felt no less painful.

"That's a big chunk of information to withhold, knowing the feelings that were growing between us." His posture turned stiff, his words even stiffer.

She twisted her hands together before her. "It's such a personal issue and so painful that I could never find the opportunity to bring it up."

He rose from the sofa, walked to the window, then stood, hands on hips, looking out into the night. "I don't know what upsets me more—the fact that you didn't trust me enough to tell me or the fact that you compare me with your ex-husband."

"I don't!"

He turned to face her. "You do. You think I'm going to react the way he did, so you don't give me a chance to be me."

"Believe me, Paul doesn't hold a candle to you. You genuinely love children. To him they were trophies. You have been immeasurably kind to the Hadaways. He ignored my work. He treated my condition with contempt. I knew you wouldn't...but, Hank, I know how much you want children of your own. You've told me time and time again." She looked down at her hands. "I vowed that I'd never become involved with a man unless he wished to remain childless or he was committed to adoption."

"And you didn't give me a chance to consider those options."

"Those options run counter to your nature."

He grasped her upper arms. Leaned close. Spoke raggedly. "You hold that opinion without ever consulting me."

She tried to hold his gaze. Tried to be brave. "I asked you what you thought about adoption—"

"That was when I thought there wasn't a need. When I thought you—"

"When you thought I was normal. Whole. Capable." She pulled away from him. "Is that what you were going to say?"

"You're putting words in my mouth again."

She looked long and hard at him, and although she saw not the faintest trace of contempt, she thought she saw pity. She couldn't bear his pity.

"This is not going to work between us," she said at last.

"It's not going to work because you're determined it shouldn't."

"Tell me honestly that you'd be willing to forgo a family."

"Never."

"That you'd be willing to adopt."

"You haven't given me much time to consider that option, Neesa. But it stands in a whole new light when I think about it with you."

She inhaled sharply, not wanting to cling to the shred of hope he offered. "The fact is that I can't give you a complete relationship in the traditional sense. You might say you don't mind now, in the beginning when passion clouds thinking, but what about down the road—"

"There won't be a down the road if we don't start a relationship with honesty and trust." He looked as if he might reach out to touch her, but he didn't. "That's what this is all about. Honesty and trust. Not genes." He sighed mightily. "Do you trust me, Neesa? You said you did earlier. Do you now?"

"I trusted you enough to tell you." Her words sounded small.

"I think it was more that you were warning me off." He narrowed his eyes. "It felt less like sharing and more like goodbye."

Perhaps he was right. If it hadn't been for that moment of what looked like pity in his eyes, she might stay and fight for him. But she didn't want his pity. Not now. Certainly not later when the honeymoon had faded. Pity had a nasty habit of turning to resentment. Perhaps he was right again with the trust issue. Perhaps she could trust him, but could she trust herself to let go of the painful issue of her own infertility? It had been a constant companion for over a year now. Could it be that she'd used it to ward off intimacy?

"I'd better go," she said.

"No." He did reach out then to touch her. Lightly, quickly on the hand. "If we don't settle this tonight, I'll be gone for a week."

"Perhaps we both need a cooling-off period."

"I don't need to cool off…I need you."

She needed him, too.

Feeling traitorous tears sting the back of her eyes, she turned from him. This needing that came with the start of relationships was so powerful. So confusing. It clouded reason.

"Neesa, don't shut me out."

"Can you promise me—"

"My promises are limited. I don't have a crystal ball that can see into the future." He put his hand on her shoulder to turn her so that she faced him. "I can't promise you how I'll feel in the end about adoption. I can't promise you that we'll live happily ever after, because I can't even promise that we won't disagree, on something, on a daily basis. Call me a realist." His face had taken on an anguished expression. "But I can promise you that I'll give this relationship my all—every day, one step at a time. I can promise honesty and trust on my part. Maybe as we move on, I can make more promises. But for now know that I need you. I want you."

"I do know that," she said softly, unable to bring herself to tell him that she felt the same. She didn't know, however, if he would come to regret even the promises he now felt comfortable making. "But I need a little space."

His stance became rigid. "We'll talk when I get back then."

She moved to leave.

"Neesa?"

"Yes?"

"Promise me one thing."

"If I can."

"Don't see yourself as a victim."

His words struck deep within her. Was that what she'd been clinging to?

Chapter Eleven

Hank stood on the veranda steps, waiting impatiently for Neesa and the Hadaways to arrive for the day. Up in the north Georgia mountains he'd worked overtime to finish up his logging contract one day early so that he wouldn't miss the regular Kids & Animals Tuesday. He hadn't seen Neesa for a whole week. He hadn't talked to her since the night she'd told him about her infertility and had, to his mind, tried to push him out of her life. He'd called her every night that he was on the road, had left messages each time on her infernal machine when she hadn't answered in person.

She hadn't returned any of his calls.

As each day passed, he'd grown more and more determined that he wasn't about to let Neesa Little slip away without some strenuous objections on his part. He might have let the matter drop if she'd said that she didn't care for him. But she hadn't. That fact gave him hope.

But at the moment, hope had been overridden by pessimism. If she and he couldn't communicate, they couldn't be honest with each other. If they couldn't be honest with each other, they couldn't begin to build trust. How many relationships had floundered because of a lack of communication, honesty and trust?

"You and Neesa have a fight?" Willy sidled up next to him.

"A misunderstanding." Hank scowled up the lane, willing the agency van to appear. "Why do you ask?"

The foreman hemmed and hawed uneasily before he replied. "It's just that Friday she brought another woman with her. Nice lady. Grandmotherly. Good with the Hadaway kids. Said she had experience on a ranch when she was younger."

"And?" Hank didn't like the direction this turn of events could take.

"Well, neither of 'em said anything outright…but I got the feeling deep down in my bones, you know, that Miss Neesa was training this woman as her replacement."

"At the agency?" Shock rippled through Hank. Neesa's devotion to the agency was all too evident for her to be considering leaving for another job.

"I didn't so much suspect her wanting to leave the agency as Whispering Pines." Scuffing the toe of his boot in the dirt, Willy didn't look at Hank. The whole set of his shoulders was one of dejection. "I got the feeling she wouldn't move the Hadaways but that she wouldn't be coming here with 'em any longer."

Damn. She wouldn't take the coward's way out and just not see him again. Would she?

"You say you never really heard them talk about any altered plans in scheduling?" Hank didn't want to think that Neesa had used their week away as the beginning of a long and permanent separation. "Maybe she's found another sponsor for a new group of children. Maybe this woman is going to be heading up that group."

Maybe but not likely. He knew the trouble she had finding him for the pilot program.

"I sure hope so." Willy sighed. "Neesa's a keeper."

"Don't I know it." Hank patted the old man on the shoulder. "And I'm going to do everything in my power to keep her."

The agency van rumbled up the lane. Even from a distance Hank could see that Neesa wasn't at the wheel. His heart sank lower than the belly of a snake.

It was only the fresh and eager faces of the five Hadaways as they tumbled out of the van that kept him from getting in his truck and chasing after Neesa. Right now. But the kids' enthusiasm was catching. Even Martin had lost some of the chip on his shoulder as he stood aside, watching the other four surround Hank.

"This is Miss Earline," Nell offered. "She was raised on a ranch in Texas."

Thomas jumped up and down. "Today Miss Reba's gonna show us all how to make sticky buns!"

"Not Martin," Rebecca corrected. "Tucker says he's gotta pull stumps with the men."

"Didja bring the big horses back?" Carlie asked. "We missed you," she added, not waiting for Hank to answer her first question.

"I missed y'all too. But I brought each of you a sack of penny candy from a funny little general store up near where I was working."

"You brought us a present?" Carlie seemed incredulous.

"Not a present so much as a reminder that you were in my thoughts."

"What did you bring Miss Neesa?" Rebecca asked.

"He brought her himself," Willy said with a catch in his voice. "Now quit your jawin' and get to the kitchen table. We got plannin' to do. There are more chores besides sticky buns and stumps today."

The four younger Hadaways followed Willy as if he were the Pied Piper. Only Martin hesitated, throwing Hank a questioning glance.

The grandmotherly woman held out her hand. "I'm Earline Johnson."

"Hank Whittaker." He shook her hand. "Neesa didn't say she was fixing to find a replacement so soon."

"Oh, she couldn't say enough about you and your ranch. I'm sure she hated to leave. But she said Whispering Pines was such a terrific opportunity for the Hadaways that she wanted to throw herself into the search for other such situations."

He just bet she did.

He forced a smile. "Well, let's head for the daily planning meeting before all the easy chores are taken."

Hank sat in the shade of a scraggly pine and picked at the box lunch Reba had packed for the men. Willy, Tucker, Martin and he had worked all morning beginning to clear a little-used pasture in preparation for planting it with alfalfa.

It was just the kind of back-breaking work that didn't allow a man time to feel sorry for himself.

"Mind if I sit here?"

Looking up, Hank was surprised to discover Martin watching him.

"Take a load off."

"You want that biscuit?" Martin pointed to Hank's barely touched lunch.

Hank smiled as he handed the teenager the whole box. "Be my guest." He could remember what it was like to be growing, with a bottomless appetite.

"Did you and Miss Neesa split up?" Martin asked around a mouthful of food. "Because of us? My brother and sisters and me."

Lordy, was his face a billboard of rejection?

"I wouldn't say we'd split up."

"Had a fight?"

"You been taking interrogation lessons from Willy?"

"No." Martin shook his head with a sorrowful smile. "It's just that I know you and Miss Neesa went out on a limb to get this program started." He looked down at the ground. "Then I screwed up. And you went away for a week. And Miss Neesa got this substitute—"

"Martin, look at me, please." Hank waited until the boy complied. "I went away because I had logging business that I'd contracted for months ago. Miss Neesa got a substitute so that she can work to get more sponsors for more kids. You haven't messed up our plans."

"Have you seen her since you got back?"

"No."

"Why not?"

Hank took a deep breath. "I guess before I see her I want to figure out the best way to ask her to marry me." He glanced quickly at Martin to see his reaction.

The boy studied his hands. "You'd still do Kids & Animals?"

"We'd still do Kids & Animals." Hank smiled. "In fact I was actually thinking of you Hadaways getting more involved on Whispering Pines."

"Like summer jobs for the others?"

"More than that." Hank enjoyed the look of curiosity that blossomed in Martin's eyes.

"What?"

"I'd better wait and present it to the five of you at once." He rose with renewed hope. By just sitting down and sharing food and a few words, by reaching out, Martin had helped clear Hank's thoughts on the future. "I'm going to call a special family meeting before you leave today."

"You mean a planning meeting like the ones we have in the morning."

"No." Hank rested his arm along the teenager's shoulder. "I mean a family meeting."

When Neesa looked at the agency clock for the umpteenth time that day, she banged her shin on an open filing cabinet drawer.

"That does it," she muttered. "Time to call it a day." She sure could use a tall, cool glass of Reba's sweet tea.

But it would be Earline drinking the tea today. Earline getting the Hadaways in the van and ready to return to the home. Earline feeling the satisfaction of a full day at Whispering Pines.

While all Neesa felt was grumpy.

She shouldn't. Earline, who had volunteered around Georgia's Waiting Children for ages, had been an angel to step in and take over this wing of Kids & Animals, leaving Neesa free to expand the program. Earline had even called her a creative and brave soul.

Creative, perhaps.

Brave, never.

If Earline could see into Neesa's heart, the cheery volunteer would see mush.

It had been a week since Neesa had seen Hank. She'd saved every one of his messages, however. Had played them over and over again. Had fallen asleep to the deep, rumbling, reassuring sound of his recorded voice. There were times when he'd called that she'd had to will her hand not to reach out and pick up the receiver. She would talk to him when he came home. Tonight or tomorrow. Until then she needed to give him space to think about the bomb she'd dropped on him their last night together.

What was it he'd then said about the prospect of adoption? That it stood in a whole new light when he thought about it with her. Could she believe him? Or were those words spoken only in the afterglow of intense physical chemistry?

My, how right the chemistry felt between them.

But she was an adult and knew full well that relationships—long-term relationships—had to be built on more than just the physical.

The agency door opened, interrupting Neesa's thoughts.

She looked up to see Hank standing in the slanting light of the waning day.

"Howdy, Neesa." He removed his Stetson. With his back to the light of the storefront windows, his face was in shadow, the expression in his eyes unreadable. "Is your boss in?"

Her boss? He'd come to see her boss? To what end?

"Y-yes. She's still here." As his presence sparked that old familiar feeling of anticipation, she made her feet move across the large front room to the office at the back. Before she announced Hank, she said to him with as much equanimity as she could muster, "I didn't expect you back until tonight or tomorrow."

"Oh, I got back last night." He studied her face. Up close, his eyes still revealed nothing. "In time to help Earline and the kids today." Was that a zinger?

He'd come home last night and he hadn't called her. He'd spent the day with the Hadaways and hadn't called her. And now he'd come to her work place...asking to see her boss.

Jill Echols's voice came from the inner office. "Neesa, is there something you wanted?"

Neesa snapped back into professional mode. "Yes. Mr. Hank Whittaker to see you."

Hank moved past her, then slowly but deliberately closed the door behind him.

Was he here to complain about Kids & Animals? Her own performance with the program perhaps? Had Martin pulled another stunt? Was Earline able to handle the five?

Oh, dear.

Because she'd moved beyond the supervision of the program at Whispering Pines, did Hank see it as abandonment? Would he now feel free to drop his end of the bargain?

Balling her fists until the knuckles showed white, Neesa marched to her own desk, a dozen negative thoughts swirling in her head. "Think positively!" she muttered. "If they'd only let me into the meeting I could explain my actions."

But that would mean publicly explaining her feelings for Hank.

She'd taken herself off Whispering Pines so there would

be no hint of impropriety. In an extreme moment of optimism, she'd wanted to leave herself free—in her personal life—to explore a relationship with Hank if, after a week apart, he decided he wanted the same.

She'd been waiting until tonight to call his house and tell him so.

But it seemed, as had been the case with Hank from the start, she'd delayed declaring her intentions until it just might be too late.

Dare she interrupt his meeting with Jill?

At that moment the door to Jill's office opened. With an inscrutable nod to Neesa, Hank walked across the outer room toward the front door.

"Neesa, would you step into my office, please?" Jill's face held no hint of what was to come.

Dear Lord, was she about to be fired? Reprimanded? Had she ruined all she'd worked for?

Trying to keep a positive attitude despite the trepidation in her heart, she walked into Jill's office.

"Please, take a seat," her boss said. "I'll be with you in a minute." And then she too disappeared.

It proved to be the longest minute in Neesa's life. Her palms grew clammy. Her hairline itched. Her pulse picked up. She nervously tapped the toes of her pumps on the floor beneath her chair.

And then Hank, of all people, reentered the room with an enormous bouquet of flowers tied with a calico ribbon. He solemnly laid them on Jill's desk, then turned to Neesa.

"Hank!" She jumped to her feet, then blurted out, "Can I call you later? I'd like to talk."

He sat on the edge of Jill's desk, so that now he and Neesa were eye-to-eye. "I might be busy later. I can spare a couple minutes now." He crossed his arms over his chest, and something…something vaguely like mischief… sparked in the depths of his eyes.

Neesa shook her head. Tension must have her seeing things.

"What was it you wanted to talk about?"

"Oh..." She tapped her fingers against her thighs. "Only a million things, really." She knew she should jump right in with the personal, but she had to know if the Hadaways still had a program come Friday. "Were the kids all right today?"

"Fine." One corner of his mouth twitched. "Fact is, Martin and I actually sat side by side to eat lunch. Spoke maybe a half-dozen civil words to each other."

"No!" She wished she'd been there to witness the breakthrough.

"Yup." His reticence wasn't making this particularly easy for her.

"Have you made plans for Friday?" She needed to know that ditching Kids & Animals wasn't his order of business earlier with Jill. "With the kids, I mean."

"Oh, sure. A full schedule. Earline took charge of the planning meeting. She's a corker." He seemed to suppress a grin. "She might even make Reba sit up and take notice where Willy's concerned."

"Is that so...?" Neesa's thoughts drifted to how the program—and Hank—appeared to be doing just fine without her.

"You wouldn't have a mind to talk about last Tuesday night, would you?" Hank's forthright question jolted her.

"Would you?" she asked, even more flustered if that were possible.

"If you go first." Darn him. He was forcing her into honesty and communication. Scary.

She took a deep breath. It was now or never. What was the worst that could happen? He could say he never wanted to see her again. She shivered at the thought.

"I've been thinking of the very last thing you said to me," she began.

"Which was?"

"You cautioned me not to take on the role of the victim."

"It doesn't become you. You're too strong a woman."

She stood in front of him, feeling open and vulnerable. "Do you know that you are the only person to ever suggest I might be feeling victimized by my infertility? Not even Claire dared to suggest it. My first reaction was anger at your insensitivity."

"I'm more interested in your second reaction. After you had time to think."

She hesitated. She had to remember that she did trust this man. He'd proven himself trustworthy. "The more I thought about it…and you…the more I wondered that maybe you didn't view my infertility as a disability. Maybe you saw it as just a part of me. Of who I am."

"Bingo," he said, his voice low, his regard more intense than she'd ever seen it. "I only wished you'd trusted me enough to share that information sooner."

"It's so painful. So personal."

"So was your divorce. But you shared that with me."

He was right. And divorce was a more external, more arbitrary circumstance.

"I guess I was afraid," she admitted.

"Why?"

"Because the stakes were so high."

"Now we're getting somewhere," he said, reaching out to clasp her hands in his. "Why were the stakes too high?" He seemed determined to press her into revealing all.

She looked down at their clasped hands. Nothing could feel as good as his renewed touch. She looked up, directly into his eyes. "Because I'd fallen in love with you."

A slow, sexy grin lit his handsome features. *"Had?"*

"Have," she corrected and felt herself blush furiously.

"Well, now, Miss Neesa Little, I love you, too—"

"You do?"

"Yes, ma'am. But there's a problem."

He didn't love her enough. He accepted her infertility, yes, but an infertile woman didn't fit into his future. Her heart felt winter chilled. She lowered her gaze.

He lifted her chin so that she had to look at him.

"I'd like to ask you to marry me," he said, "but I've made plans for a big family."

Yes, of course. She would have to steel herself to loving him enough to let him go. It was only fair.

He reached behind him. From the desktop he presented her with the bouquet of flowers. "You see, I have this ready-made family. Five kids. It isn't every woman who wants to be a bride and an instant mom."

What was he talking about?

He nudged the flowers in her direction.

With trembling hands, she accepted the bouquet. Glancing into the mix of blossoms, she realized it was no florist's arrangement. No, these were wildflowers. Daisies. Lilies. Black-eyed Susans. Honeysuckle. Wild grasses. The kind that flourished on Whispering Pines.

"Did you pick these yourself?"

"I had help. Look closer."

She did, and saw, tucked amid the blooms, five photos. The kind that Georgia's Waiting Children stapled to their clients' file folders. These were specifically of Martin, Nell, Thomas, Carlie and Rebecca. Faces more dear to her even than the hand-picked flowers that framed them.

Her thoughts whirring too fast for comprehension, she looked back up at Hank. "What does this mean?"

"It's a long story." He grinned at her as if there were no tomorrow. "But you'd better hear it all before I ask you to marry me."

"Marry you..." One hand fluttered to her heart.

"You know how much I want a family. Well, there are these five terrific kids who need a dad...and a mom, too, but I don't have the final say in that. I met these kids through a great program. Kids & Animals. Perhaps you've heard of it?"

She grinned up at him like a fool, hardly daring to hope. "These kids have just fallen in love with Whispering

Pines." He faltered, his voice growing gruff, his eyes misty. "And I have to admit I've fallen in love with them."

Neesa's heart purely melted.

"So I asked them today if they'd like to take a stab at making a family."

"You didn't!"

"I did. Although it complicates my life."

"How so?"

"There's this woman I love beyond reason. I want to ask her to marry me."

Neesa felt tears of joy sting her eyes. "What's the complication?"

"It seems that when the paperwork is finished...I just got it rolling with Ms. Echols...I'll be a single dad with five kids. I'm not sure whether any sane woman would want to take on a marriage and *other people's children*." He cocked one eyebrow.

"Then call me crazy!" Neesa flung her arms around his neck. "You impossible man!"

He skewered her with a smoky look. "You heard me tell Martin I purely hate the word *impossible*."

"Then let me hear the possibilities."

He wrapped his arms around her. Pulled her close. "If we can convince Reba, Willy and Tucker to baby-sit, we might catch us a honeymoon."

"Don't you think you've just put the cart before the mule?"

"Ah, yes." He went very still, his gaze bathing her in exquisite tenderness. "Neesa Little, I love you. Will you marry me?"

"I love you right back," she replied with rising joy. Her heart refused to beat at a regular pace. "And, yes, I'll marry you."

The expression on his face seemed to say he could gobble her up.

Oh, my.

He lowered his lips to hers and swept her up in a passionate kiss like none they'd shared before. This kiss was more than chemistry. This kiss was backed with honest acceptance and trust and hope for the future. This kiss promised the simplicity of hot nights in a marriage bed and the complications of ironing out the ever-present wrinkles of family life during the cool of day. This kiss was promise and fulfillment and the unexpected all rolled into one.

Neesa felt the prickle of anticipation clear down to her toes.

Clutching the precious bouquet in one hand, she ran the fingers of the other through his hair and deepened the kiss. At once, she inhaled the scent of flowers and fresh air and Hank.

Hank. The most wonderful man in the whole world.

And soon to be her husband.

The father of her children.

In the most unexpected of quarters, Neesa Little had found love—and a family—for keeps.

Epilogue

Several months later

The gray light of dawn filled the barn as Hank, ripping open a fresh bag of mash, caught his wedding band on a loose nail sticking out from the side of the feed storage bin. He knew some ranchers never wore their rings during the work-filled day.

But Hank never intended to take this one off. Ever.

"What all have you finished?" Martin's sleepy voice made him smile. The boy seemed to relish early mornings as much as Hank. At least he was always up at the crack of dawn, always attentive to the ranch animals' needs.

Like father, like son.

After today, Hank could officially say that. Today the final adoption papers would be signed, making Neesa and him parents. Making the Hadaways Whittakers. Making them all a family.

"I just got out here myself," Hank replied. "I guess feeding's the top of the order. Although we're running low on mash for the horses."

Martin grabbed a bucket. "I'll talk Willy into letting me drive to town. I need the practice." The teenager's words were as clear and as matter-of-fact as the click of a clock. It was amazing how his hostility had vaporized in the past few months.

"Make sure you're back in plenty of time for the party."

"Oh, I wouldn't miss this one." The boy grinned from ear to ear. A wholly satisfying sight.

Neesa and Reba had a big party planned for the afternoon. They'd invited Willy and Tucker, of course. And Earline who was now working on a dairy farm with another group from Kids & Animals. And Jill Echols. And Evan, Cilla, Chris and Casey Russell. And Hank's brother Brett, plus some reporter who was dogging him, doing a week-in-the-life-of-a-county-sheriff article. And a slew of kids from the state home, kids the Hadaways had known from their former life.

It was going to be a blow-out party, but chores didn't know anything about parties. They needed doing seven days a week. Hank knew he was lucky he had a big family who would run through this morning's ranch routine lickety-split.

"Papa?" Rebecca popped up next to him, her nightshirt hastily tucked into a miniature pair of jeans.

"Yes, sunshine." Rebecca's use of "Papa" brought a lump to his throat every time. She had immediately clung to the idea of Neesa and him as parents. And now, of the five children, only Martin still called him Hank.

"You gonna help blow up balloons?" She fisted her hand to rub sleep from her eyes.

"After breakfast. Are you going to feed Miss Kitty and her mutant ninja teenagers?"

"Yup." She giggled at his silliness as she climbed on a low stool to reach the cat chow.

Willy, Tucker and Thomas came into the barn. "We're going to get the stalls mucked out and out of the way," Willy said. "Miss Neesa wants you in the kitchen."

And he wanted her. Every minute of every day.

"Hey, Pop," Thomas called over his shoulder. "Uncle Brett said he'd give me a ride in his cruiser this afternoon. Said he'd let me sound the siren."

"Just what we need on this ranch." Hank grinned, heading out of the barn toward his wife. "More confusion."

But he felt blessed. Yes, sir, he did.

Carlie waved good morning from the chicken yard where she scattered meal for the hens.

Nell, as she came across the dew-streaked pasture, held up a basket. "Blackberries, Dad!" she called out loud and clear. "For breakfast!"

His mouth watered in anticipation.

And then his heart nearly stopped as Neesa—his wife and mother of his children—stepped out on the utility porch off the kitchen. The petite blonde still didn't look as if she belonged on a ranch. She still looked as if she should be hosting society charity events. Even in a T-shirt and blue jeans she seemed china-doll fragile. Oh, but he knew the strength of her.

Ignoring the steps, he leaped up onto the porch and pulled her into a bear hug. "Heard you had need of my services." He nuzzled her neck.

Laughing, she ran her hands down his sides. "Later, cowboy. Right now I want to talk to you about a proposition I'd like to lay down before the kids at breakfast."

"Does this proposition happen to have two arms, two legs and need of a foster home?"

She grinned up at him. "Two arms, two legs and wheels. Teresa uses a wheelchair."

"Why are you asking me?" He looked at her with mock helplessness. "My hands are tied without a family counsel. You'll have to bring it up at breakfast, *Roberts Rules of Order* and all."

"I am hungry," she murmured far too sexily for a mother of five.

"Me, too."

He kissed her then. Full and hard and in view of his ever-expanding family. He didn't know what would be decided at this morning's breakfast meeting. All he knew was what Neesa had taught him: the human heart was capable of expanding to love any and all who needed it.

* * * * *

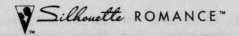

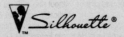

This March Silhouette is proud to present

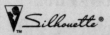

Silhouette®

SENSATIONAL

MAGGIE SHAYNE
BARBARA BOSWELL
SUSAN MALLERY
MARIE FERRARELLA

This is a special collection of four complete
novels for one low price, featuring a novel
from each line: Silhouette Intimate Moments,
Silhouette Desire, Silhouette Special Edition
and Silhouette Romance.

Available at your favorite retail outlet.

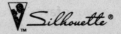

Silhouette®

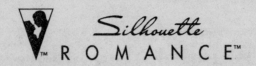

COMING NEXT MONTH

#1348 THE NIGHT BEFORE BABY—Karen Rose Smith
Loving the Boss

The rumors were true! Single gal Olivia McGovern was pregnant, and dashing Lucas Hunter was the father-to-be. So the honorable lawyer offered to marry Olivia for the baby's sake. But time spent in Olivia's loving arms had her boss looking for more than just "honor" from his wedded wife!

#1349 A VOW, A RING, A BABY SWING—Teresa Southwick
Bundles of Joy

Pregnant and alone, Rosie Marchetti had just been stood up at the altar. So family friend Steve Schafer stepped up the aisle and married her. And although Steve thought he wasn't good enough for the shy beauty, she was out to convince him that this family was meant to be....

#1350 BABY IN HER ARMS—Judy Christenberry
Lucky Charm Sisters

Josh McKinney had found his infant girl. Now he had to find a baby expert—quick! So he convinced charming Maggie O'Connor to take care of little Ginny. But the more time Josh spent with his temporary family, the more he wanted to make Maggie his real wife....

#1351 NEVER TOO LATE FOR LOVE—Marie Ferrarella
Like Mother, Like Daughter

CEO Bruce Reed thought his life was full—until he met the flirtatious Margo McCloud at his son's wedding. Her sultry voice permeated his dreams, and he wondered if his son had the right idea about marriage. But could he convince Margo that it wasn't too late for their love?

#1352 MR. RIGHT NEXT DOOR—Arlene James
He's My Hero

Morgan Holt was everything Denise Jenkins thought a hero should be—smart, sexy, intelligent—and he had swooped to her rescue by pretending to be her beloved. But if Morgan was busy saving Denise, who was going to save Morgan's heart from *her* once their romance turned real?

#1353 A FAMILY FOR THE SHERIFF—Elyssa Henry
Family Matters

Fall for a sheriff? Never! Maria Lightner had been hurt by doing that once before. But when lawman Joe Roberts strolled into her life, Maria took another look. And even though her head said he was wrong, her heart was telling her something altogether different....